STARTING TROUBLE

Collier's hand came up out of nowhere and slapped Lane on the cheek.

Sedley called out from down the bar. "Hey, none of that in here."

"That's fine," said Collier. "We're takin' it outside." He motioned with his hat toward the door. "Go ahead."

Lane stepped into the cold night, where light flakes were still falling. He couldn't see a way out of this one. The last thing he was going to do was let someone call him a coward. Even if it meant—

Collier's fist caught him before he had even decided how to square off. His feet went out from under him on the slick sidewalk, and he landed with his rump on the boards.

"Get up."

He shifted up onto his elbows, in no hurry for the next part.

"Get up, you pot-licker." Collier leaned over, grabbed him by the front of his coat, and jerked him to his feet. The next punch put him in the street.

Lane's cheek and jaw throbbed with a sharp ache, and the world was tilted. Collier hauled him up again. This time he punched him in the stomach....

Other *Leisure* books by John D. Nesbitt:

RANCHO ALEGRE
WEST OF ROCK RIVER
RED WIND CROSSING
BLACK HAT BUTTE
FOR THE NORDEN BOYS
MAN FROM WOLF RIVER
NORTH OF CHEYENNE
COYOTE TRAIL
WILD ROSE OF RUBY CANYON
BLACK DIAMOND RENDEZVOUS
ONE-EYED COWBOY WILD

Lonesome Range

JOHN D. NESBITT

LEISURE BOOKS NEW YORK CITY

For Will Baker.

A LEISURE BOOK®

June 2006

Published by

Dorchester Publishing Co., Inc.
200 Madison Avenue
New York, NY 10016

ISBN 0-8439-5541-4

Printed in the United States of America.

Lonesome
Range

Chapter One

It began with two horses. A house at the edge of town, a woman standing at the window looking out at two children, her glance lifting to the man who rode one horse and led another.

A man with the reins in one hand and a lead rope in the other, braced in the chill of sunlight. Far country flung away in all directions, a book he was yet to read.

The breeze came in off the plains, carrying the scent of sagebrush, dry grass, damp earth. The ring of eight shod hooves rising from the packed road mixed with the undertone of the children's soft voices and, from somewhere, not too far out in the prairie, the tinkling notes of a meadowlark.

The fence in front of the yard moved along on his right, and up ahead, across the west end of the yard, he could see a fringe of young cedar trees, where the rust color of winter was giving way to green. As he brought the horses to a stop, his eyes went back to the woman's, and she looked down—something on the air and then no more, gone like a stone dropped into a pond.

When he came to the gate he swung down, transferred the lead rope, and gathered the reins. Motion caught his eye, and he saw the woman at the front door.

"Good afternoon," he called across the distance. "Are you Mrs. McGavin?"

"Yes, I am."

"My name's Lane Weller. I've got a horse for your husband. My employer, Mr. St. John, sent it over. He said he thought Mr. McGavin would be home."

The woman spoke as she came closer. "I'm not sure where he is. He stepped out for a few minutes. I'm sure he'll be back in a little while." She turned her head to the side and in a softer tone said, "Don't pull on his ears."

Lane followed her glance to the two children, a dark-haired boy and a light-haired girl, who had a brown puppy on the grass between them. Then he looked at the woman, who came to a stop about eight feet away.

He noticed her dark hair, then her eyes, which seemed a grayish green, and her clear complexion. She had some color to her—not pale, as most women were when they had spent the winter inside.

"Where do you think I should put him?" Lane motioned with his head toward the bareback horse.

The woman moved her mouth, neither frowning

nor smiling. Her gaze went to the horse and then back to Lane. "You can just leave him with me. I'll find some place to tie him, and when my husband comes back, he can take him to the stable."

"Well, if I had known—"

She shook her head. "No, that's all right." Her face relaxed into a smile, showing clean, even teeth. "I'm not afraid of horses. I grew up around them."

"That should be fine, then." He stepped back as she walked toward the gate, and as she opened it and came through, he thought she had a nice figure beneath her apron.

Their eyes met as he handed her the lead rope. Then as she took the rope and lowered her eyelids, he saw that she had dark, pretty lashes. He searched for more to say, but he couldn't find it.

She raised her eyes to look at him again. "I'm sure my husband will be glad to have the horse. And it's been a pleasure to meet you, Mr.—"

"Weller. Lane Weller. But you can call me Lane." He felt his pulse jump. "Actually, I'd prefer it."

Her eyes sparkled, as if they were about to mist over. "I think I can bring myself to do that, provided that you call me Cora."

He smiled. "I think I can do that."

She gave him her hand and said, "It's nice to meet you, and thank you again."

He felt the touch, pressed with his thumb, and then released her hand. "Nice, indeed, and I hope to see you again before long." He edged his horse back and away, tipped his hat, and mounted up.

The picket fence moved on his left, and he caught a glimpse of the two children with the puppy. Fifty yards out, he nudged the horse into a quarter turn and looked back. The woman was still standing at the gate, and when he waved, she raised her hand and waved back.

Cora. Nicest-looking woman he had seen since he left Cheyenne, but all tied up with marriage and kids. How else would she come to a place like this? Nice surprise when she smiled. Said she wasn't afraid of horses. Pretty eyes, and eyelashes. Just the slightest bit of color to her, too. Maybe somewhere, who knows how far back, a French trapper or a gray-back farm boy met a pretty Indian girl. Sure no harm in that. Damn the luck, though. She was a true rose in the desert.

Lane was busy transcribing a letter when the front door of the office opened and Joseph Saxton walked in. He took off his hat, a high-crowned, narrow-brimmed affair, and stood in front of Lane's desk.

"Good afternoon, Joseph. Something I can do for you?"

Saxton hesitated, hat in both hands, giving Lane a moment to scan the beady eyes and thin nose, high forehead and dark, wavy hair. The man always had a serious, deliberate air about him, as if his world did not have enough latitude for business and pleasure both.

"You know Mrs. Apley, don't you?"

"Mrs. Apley? No, I can't say that I do."

"Apley, I say. Emma Apley. You know her husband, Douglas, at least."

"Well, of course I know him. St. John buys from him. I believe I just paid a bill for some harness parts the other day—a singletree, actually, and not the harness itself. Something that one of the men needed up north."

"Good enough. As you may know, they have me to dinner about once a week. Nothing formal."

"Uh-huh."

"And in the course of conversation, Emma and I—Mrs. Apley, that is—thought it might be fitting, or pleasant, if some of us who shared similar interests might get together once in a while. Relieve the tedium, you know."

"Sure."

"And we thought you might like to join us."

"I'm very flattered. But I'm not sure what you have in mind—a quilting bee, or something more like a thespian society?"

"Oh, I'm sorry. I could have been more specific. Our primary line of interest so far has been literature. Talk about the things we have read."

"The great novels? Shakespeare? I enjoy all of those things, of course."

"I knew you like to read, and when Emma suggested that we form a little group, your name came up as well."

"It sounds like a pleasure. When do you think you might have your first meeting?"

The eyebrows went up over the beady eyes. "Tomorrow evening, if it's not too soon. That's the best time for Mrs. Apley. I, of course, have an open calendar."

"As do I."

A nod. "Say about seven?"

"Where the place? Upon the heath?"

Saxton made a tight smile of acknowledgment. "At Mrs. Apley's."

"Bring anything?"

Now he gave an expression that passed for an arch smile. "Your volume of Shakespeare, which you seem so fond of. You could give us Marc Antony's funeral oration."

"Oh, I wouldn't need the text for that."

"Well enough. Bring your compendious memory."

"Caesar, I shall."

Saxton tipped his head, gave the tight smile again, and put on his hat as he turned away. He went out the door and closed it behind him. Lane watched as he passed by the window and out of sight.

Back to the store, no doubt, to weigh out beans and measure yards of muslin. Not the worst sort to be matched with in the brotherhood of bachelors. For the most part he kept to himself in the store and in the living quarters behind. If he had an idea for a soirée, no harm in that.

Lane recognized the woman who opened the front door. He had seen her on the street. Closer now, he took in her blue eyes and light brown hair, light complexion and open expression. She wore a white blouse with dark blue trim that matched her skirt.

"Mrs. Apley?" He took off his hat.

"Yes, Mr. Weller. So very nice of you to come." She gave him her hand and then stepped back to let him into the front room.

Joseph Saxton was sitting at the left end of the sofa. Lane nodded to him and said hello as he stepped into the middle of the room. Then something caught the corner of his eye, and his pulse quickened as he turned to see Cora McGavin standing in the kitchen doorway.

She wore a high-necked red blouse with black piping; half a dozen black buttons ran down a tapering placket in front. A full-length black skirt reached her shoes. With a quick glance he was able to confirm his earlier impression that she had a trim figure.

"How do you do?" he asked.

"Very well."

"Nice to see you again."

"I think we all know each other," came Mrs. Apley's voice from behind. "Feel free to take a seat. I need to look after the baby."

Cora moved across the room and sat at the unoccupied end of the sofa. Lane pulled a wooden sitting chair around perpendicular to her and away from the low table that sat in front of the sofa. He caught a view of her lowered eyelids, as before, and let his gaze rove. Then he found himself pausing at the buttons on her blouse, and he made himself look away.

"How go the wars, Joseph?"

"As well as could be expected. And yourself?"

"About the same."

Mrs. Apley appeared at the kitchen doorway with a baby in her arms. "This is Trixie," she said, stepping forward. "She's about to go to bed. Her papa is going to sit with her for a while and read a newspaper, so nobody will be bothered."

The proud mother showed the baby to Joseph, to Cora, and then to Lane. It was a normal-looking baby, with a vacant blue gaze and a slobbery lower lip.

"This is Mr. Weller, Trixie. Say hello."

Trixie, still a long ways from that point in the journey at which she would be able to say hello, lolled her head.

Lane raised his eyebrows and gave a wide stare at the baby. Getting no response, he said, "Cute name."

"Short for Beatrice, of course." The woman shifted the bundle in her arms. "Well, now that she's said good night to everybody, she can go be with her papa."

As Mrs. Apley left the room, Lane glanced at Joseph, who seemed to be as far removed from the experience of babies as he was. Then he turned to Cora.

"Probably not so long ago when your own children were as small as that."

She smiled. "Seems like no time at all. And the first one, of course, like Emma now, to have your own baby in your arms—"

"Oh, I'm sure." Lane nodded and looked at Joseph.

"No doubt," said the storekeeper. "A bit of bliss that everybody can hope for."

Silence hung in the air for a moment. Lane was trying to keep himself from staring at Cora, but he did not want to seem to be ignoring her, either. When he did turn his eyes toward her, he found her looking at him.

"So where are you from originally, if I may ask, Mr. Weller?"

"Pennsylvania."

She turned to the other man present. "Oh, that's not so far from Ohio."

"Actually," said Lane, "I come from the eastern part of the state. A little town called Clarks Summit, not far from Scranton. Way north of Philadelphia."

"I see. And what part of Ohio are you from, Joseph?"

"A town called Marion." He made a small wave with his hand. "Nothing famous about it."

Lane caught himself looking at the buttons again. He lifted his gaze and noticed that her hair, which had been pinned up during their first meeting, was now combed back and banded but hung loose. "And yourself, Mrs. McGavin? And by the way, shouldn't we just go by first name?"

Her eyes met his. "Of course."

"Anyway," he resumed, "won't you tell us where you're from, if the question is not too indiscreet?"

She smiled. "Not at all. I'm from Nebraska."

"Oh. Uh-huh. I think you mentioned the other day that you were raised around horses."

"Yes, I grew up on ranches."

"Do you rope cattle?" He wagged his eyebrows.

She laughed. "Not much."

Mrs. Apley came into the room with a swish of skirts and stopped short. "Well, I've got Trixie put away, so I think we can go ahead. Let me get another chair."

Lane stood up and offered her his seat.

"Not at all," she said. "I'll pull one around." She walked to the window, where the curtains were drawn together, and laid her hand on a lightweight rocking chair. Then with a turn she said, "Joseph, would you mind?"

Saxton, almost bolting, rose from the sofa and crossed the room.

Lane looked at Cora. "It's nice to be able to have a little get-together like this."

"Oh, yes. The credit goes to Emma. One has to be resourceful to keep life from becoming desolate in these places."

"That seems to be the way with this country. The winter doldrums can come at any time, and one has to work out so many things by oneself."

"Right here," said Mrs. Apley.

With as much care as if he were handling a bassinet, Joseph set down the chair to form a fourth corner in the seating arrangement.

Mrs. Apley sat down, ran two fingers across her brow, and let out a breath. "Well, now, where shall we start? Mr. Weller—"

Joseph interposed. "Mr. Weller has suggested

that we all go by first name. Is that agreeable with you, Emma?"

"Yes, that's fine." She brushed at a loose hair on her temple as she looked again at Lane. "What we thought we might do is share our interests in things we have read and enjoyed. Not necessarily anything lofty, you know. Just something to keep things alive."

"Sounds fine."

"And we thought we might start, for the first meeting or two, with poetry. Joseph and I discovered that we share a fondness for the schoolroom poets, and Cora says that she has read them as well. I suppose you have, too, Mr., um, Lane?"

"Oh, yes. I enjoy them, along with many other things as well. Some more than others, of course."

"Longfellow?"

"It's been a while since I read him, but his work stays with a person. Some of the scenes from 'Evangeline,' for example, or even 'The Courtship of Miles Standish.' Rather stirring, some of it." He looked at Cora. "What do you think?"

"Oh, 'Evangeline.' Who hasn't read it and felt something?"

"Well," said Joseph, "I imagine many people haven't read it at all. This country is full of them—men and women both—who can barely read the label on a liniment bottle."

Cora's face colored for an instant. "I know for a fact that a great many people haven't read it, but what I meant was that people who do read it feel the sorrow." She turned to Lane. "Don't you think so?"

"Oh, yes. Indeed. And the meter is noble. 'This is the forest primeval, the murmuring pines and hemlocks . . .' "

"Go on," said Emma. "A few more lines."

"I know but the first two or three, that's all."

"Don't be so modest," said Joseph. "I'm sure you could give us the whole poem if we were willing to sit through it."

"Not that one. Maybe something shorter, like a couplet from Pope."

"I think you're like a stone in the desert," Joseph returned. "If we tapped you with a rod, the verses would flow like a river. Whole scenes from Shakespeare, all of *Paradise Lost*."

"Maybe 'Who Killed Cock Robin?' or 'Little Boy Blue.' "

It soon became evident that both Emma and Joseph were willing to recite poetry and that Emma, with a subtle hand, had brought them back to Longfellow as the theme of the evening. After a moment of ceremonious hesitation, she stood up and delivered "The Village Blacksmith." Following that, Joseph took the floor and gave the company a full declamation of "Paul Revere's Ride."

Lane, who had memorized both poems in his boyhood, took pleasure in following along. But when the group's attention turned to him, he pleaded a lack of preparation.

Cora did likewise. It had been a long time, she

said, since she had done any reciting, and she was going to have to build up her nerve.

When the lull came, Emma and Cora got up to serve coffee and cookies. From where he sat, Lane watched Cora as she lifted blue willowware out of a glass cabinet in the kitchen. When she moved out of sight, he turned his attention to Joseph, who seemed to have drawn inward.

"Great lines," said Lane. "'Booted and spurred and ready to ride.'"

"Oh, yes."

"When I was a boy, before I was old enough to learn the poem myself, the teacher read it to us."

"Ours did, too. And I always thought it ended too soon. I wished it had more of the battles and fighting. Of course, when it came to memorizing it, it was long enough."

Cora emerged from the kitchen with a tray. On it were cups, saucers, and two plates, all of the blue willow pattern. The cups were empty, but the two plates each had a mound of pale cookies. She set the tray on the low table and stood aside as Emma poured coffee into the cups. After Emma sat down, Cora walked around behind the two chairs and took her seat on the sofa.

Lane could feel her presence when she came near, first when the bottom of her skirt brushed the leg of his chair, and then when she held a plate of cookies toward him and asked him to take at least one.

No one spoke much for the next little while except to compliment the coffee or the cookies. When all the cups had returned to the table and everyone sat back, Lane imagined the evening's event was nearing the end. Rather than leave too soon, he waited until Joseph rose from his seat. The two of them took leave of the women, Joseph taking each woman's hand, bidding her good night, and giving her a little bow. Then he stood back and watched. Lane gave his thanks to Emma for the fine evening, taking her hand in a light touch, and moved to take Cora's. As he did, his eyes met for a longer moment with hers.

"Certainly nice to meet you again, Cora."

"Yes, it was. I hope we can all get together again before long."

"We'll see what we can do about having something ready for presentation." He gave her his best smile.

Her eyes sparkled. "It's going to take more work for me, but we'll see."

The two men stepped out into the evening and walked without speaking until they came to the main street. There they wished each other good night and went their separate ways, Joseph to the right and Lane to the left. Night had fallen, but a couple of other people were out and about.

Lane headed for a patch of light that fell on the sidewalk up ahead. When he reached it, he turned left into the Last Chance Saloon.

Tom Sedley was tending bar as usual. Lane took a place halfway down the bar, put his foot on the rail, and leaned his forearm on the counter.

Tom set a mug of beer in front of him. "You look like you're in good spirits tonight."

"I hadn't thought about it, but maybe I am." Lane set a silver dollar on the bar top. In the mirror he saw himself and a couple of other patrons down the bar to his right. After a sip of his beer, he cast his glance around the saloon, taking in the familiar spread of elk antlers on the end wall and the mounted head of a longhorn on the side wall.

Tom reached into his vest pocket, drew out a toothpick, and poked at his teeth below the bushy mustache. "Any news fit to print?"

"Nah, not really." Lane took another drink. "What do you know about this fellow Lyle McGavin?"

"Not much. Land developer. Comes from the land of mules and hog meat, I think."

"Where's that?"

"Missouri."

"Huh."

"Have you got dealings with him?"

"Not much. He's been through the office a couple of times, and St. John had me deliver a horse to him."

Tom glanced around and spoke in a lower tone of voice. "A man might want to count his change if he deals with that fellow, but I imagine St. John can take care of himself."

"I think so."

"I haven't heard of anything he's done since he's been here, but he just seems like that kind."

"Uh-huh. What-all does he do?"

"A little of this and a little of that. Locate claims,

buy and sell parcels, buy up lots in town. He'll sell a lot to someone, then lend 'em the money to put up a building, and he'll hold the mortgage on it."

"Oh, I've heard of that. Sometimes they end up with the building and property both. Not the kind of fellow who would spend his time reading 'Evangeline,' then."

Tom glanced to his right. A man had just come in and taken a place at the end of the bar. "I wouldn't suspect him of it. There's not much percentage in that."

Tom walked down the bar to wait on the customer, a fellow who stood a little shorter than average and wore a dark mustache. Lane placed him—Newt Collier, a jack-of-all-trades around town. Seemed to have an eye out for everything. Lane was pretty sure he had seen him on the street a few minutes earlier.

Tom came back, fishing the toothpick out of his vest pocket again. Facing Lane but not quite square, he tapped his left forefinger against the side of his nose. Then he spoke in a normal voice. "What do you think of the way the tumbleweeds are takin' over the country?"

"Hard to know what to think."

As Tom wandered down to the other end of the bar, Lane found something to think about anyway. He entertained pleasant images of red cloth with black trim and buttons.

Chapter Two

From where he sat at his desk, Lane had a view of a short segment of the main street. From time to time he looked up from his ledgers, as much to rest his eyes as to see what little traffic Willow Springs had to offer. A team of mules or horses, hitched together, didn't have much distinction, and one freight wagon looked like another.

The door opened, and a man in dusty, wrinkled clothes walked in. He looked to be about forty, with a beard running to gray and crow's-feet at the corners of his eyes, but he stood straight and had a square set to his shoulders.

"Yes, sir?" said Lane.

"Do you know where I can find the road to the Umo Ranch?"

Lane shook his head. "I sure don't. I've never heard of it."

"The Umo Ranch. I heard they were puttin' on men."

"Might be, but I don't know where it is."

St. John's voice came from his office. "What's he want?"

Lane turned in his chair and looked back, through the open door of the inner sanctum, where St. John sat with his head raised. "He wants to know where the Umo Ranch is."

St. John stood up and came out into the main office. Tall and clean and well groomed, he made quite a contrast with the stranger as they stood six feet apart.

"The Umo Ranch, you say?"

"That's the way I heard it, and I had the man say it more'n once. I heard they were puttin' men on."

"Well, I don't know where it would be." St. John gave the man a once-over. "How are you traveling?"

The man held his brown eyes steady as he answered. "I'm on foot, but I'm not afraid to walk, if I know where it is."

St. John shook his head. "I don't think there's a place around here with that name, but there are plenty of other outfits that are startin' to hire. They'll be comin' into town, lookin' for hands."

"I'd like to go to work as soon as I could."

"Oh, I'm sure." St. John turned toward Lane. "Get a dollar out of the drawer to help this man."

Lane pulled out the bottom drawer of his desk, opened the cash box, and lifted a silver dollar with thumb and forefinger.

The stranger had an uncomfortable look on his face. "I didn't come in here lookin' for a handout."

"I know," said St. John. "But this'll help you until you find work, which I don't think will be too long."

The man took the dollar from Lane and nodded to St. John. "I thank you, sir. I'll remember you."

"You're welcome. And good luck."

The man walked out through the door, closing it with care. He bent to the sidewalk, picked up a knapsack, and walked past the window out of sight.

"Down on his luck," said Lane. "Had kind of a lonesome look to him."

"Oh, he's all right. Just ran out of money a little sooner than he expected. Maybe drank too much at some point over the winter. But he'll be back on his feet in no time, herdin' cattle or pitchin' hay."

"He looked fit for that."

"Sure he did. And if it wasn't for men like him, none of us would have a dime."

As St. John went back to his office, Lane turned over that last remark a couple of times. Then he dipped his pen in the inkwell and resumed writing in the ledger.

Shortly after the dinner hour, St. John appeared again at Lane's right.

"I need you to write a letter," he began. "Address it to Harry Templeton at the Twin Pines, out of Newcastle. Tell him I'm going to send a man up that way to make an assessment of the property he told me about. Tell him I appreciate his recommendation and look forward to this man's report."

"Should I mention the man's name?"

"Yes, do that. It's this fellow Lyle McGavin. And while you're at it, draw up a letter of introduction for him to take along."

"Address the letter of introduction specifically to Templeton as well?"

"Oh, yes. I wouldn't want someone to get the idea he could trade on my good name wherever he went."

"Good enough."

Lane went about the task of writing out the two letters in as fair a hand as possible, but he still had a few scratches and blotches. Then he moved across the office to the typing desk, next to the hat and coat rack. St. John liked to send out typed correspondence, and he seemed to like to have the typewriter in a prominent place.

The machine required hard strokes on the little round keys, and Lane had to bear down his attention to maintain accuracy at the same time that he made a good, clear impression on the page. As he was finishing the first letter, St. John took leave for the day, reminding Lane to lock up in the evening.

Lane did not ask his employer where he was going, but he supposed the man was on his way home to the house that Lane had seen only on the outside—not an ostentatious structure, but large and solid, with a rock foundation, pillars on the porch, half a dozen gables, and a couple of dormer windows. Lane imagined St. John sitting down in the parlor with his reserved wife and their two daughters, all of whom played musical instruments and did not venture often beyond the front porch.

When the second letter had made its way through the roller, Lane proofread the two typed copies, left them on the boss's desk, and filed the handwritten originals. Then he went back to work with the grain and cattle ledgers.

As the end of the workday drew near, he began to feel small tingles of anticipation. The week had come around to Thursday again, and his thoughts went forward to another evening at Emma's. All through the intervening week he had hoped to see Cora pass by the window, but she hadn't. Now it was just a matter of a couple of hours.

After locking up the office, he lost no time getting to his room, where he went over a page of poetry a few times. He had studied it all week, but after a day of clerical work, he needed to get his mind back into verses and stanzas.

Downstairs he ate a quick supper. As he was walking out of the dining room he met Madeline Edgeworth, a fellow lodger, who was on her way in. With her discreet air of the wise woman of the world, she smiled and said hello. Lane returned the greeting, then went upstairs for one more review of the text.

Lane was the first to arrive at Emma Apley's house. As she invited him in, he said, "Your lilacs are beautiful."

"Aren't they lovely? They've bloomed so well this year."

"They almost overwhelmed me with their perfume as I walked up to the door. And what are those little blue flowers that are just starting to bloom out front?"

"Oh, those are flax. When the weather warms up, the petals drop off in the heat of the day, and they put on a new set each morning. They don't take much care, and they bloom for three months or so."

"That's convenient." He stood with his hat in his hands.

"Won't you have a seat? The others won't be long, I'm sure."

"Thank you." Lane saw that the seating was arranged as before, so he sat in the same chair and bided his time as Emma moved around in the kitchen. The curtains on the front window were drawn, so he could not keep a lookout for anyone arriving.

Within a few minutes, a knock came at the door. Emma crossed the corner of the front room, and as she opened the door, Lane heard the cheery voices of both women. He rose to meet Cora as she came into the house.

She was dressed in a dark blue outfit this time, a jacket and long skirt, with a white blouse. Her dark hair hung loose to her shoulders.

Lane stepped forward to take her hand, and as she took his, he noticed that her eyes looked blue. He ascribed the effect to the color of her jacket.

Emma asked them both to be seated and then

went back into the kitchen. Cora took her place on the sofa, and Lane sat in his chair.

"Nice that you could make it again," he said.

"Oh, yes, my husband is very cooperative about letting me go to events like this, when there's so little to do in this country."

"How fortunate. As you said last time, it does become desolate at times. Yet people come here—we all did—and many of them stay. In spite of the bleakness, it's a place of great opportunity."

"Well, yes, especially for people who want to make money. So many men come to make a fortune, it seems—or at least they hope to."

"That's true. Of course, they don't all make it."

"But they try. It drives so many of them."

"Oh, yes."

Cora brushed at a piece of lint on her dress. "You don't seem to be that way, though."

"I can't say that I am."

"It would make a person wonder why you came here, then."

"Why I came? Why, to work, I guess. Like a lot of others." He shrugged and gave her a smile.

She smiled back in a comfortable way. "Yes, but you must want something more than just a job."

"Oh, I suppose I do."

With her chin on her knuckles, and her elbow on the arm of the sofa, she peered at him. "Some people don't know what they want, but I would think you do."

"I imagine I do."

She had an encouraging look on her face. "Tell me what it is. What you want."

"I don't believe I've put it in words before."

"But you're good with words. I've seen that already." Her expression was still encouraging, but it had become almost playful. "Tell me."

"Well, that's rather direct, but I think I can respond in kind. Excuse me if it sounds too embellished, but I imagine I want to find something larger than myself to believe in. There, I've said it."

She raised her eyebrows. "That was very well put. I must say, I don't hear much about things like that."

"I'm free to give it a try, anyway."

Her expression became earnest. "Please don't misunderstand me. I think it's wonderful. I just don't hear those kinds of ideas expressed very often."

He was on the brink of asking her the same question in return, when a knock sounded on the front door. Emma called out from the kitchen, and Joseph Saxton opened the door and stepped in. He paused at the kitchen to say hello to Emma, then turned his beady eyes on Lane and Cora. After a round of greetings, he took his place on the sofa.

Emma came in from the kitchen, brushing her hands on her skirt, and sat in the rocking chair. "Well, Trixie and her papa are safely stowed away, and I think we can begin."

"I have to confess," said Cora, "that I haven't been able to come up with anything in so short a time. I'm afraid I'm better at reading than I am at memorizing or reciting. But I'd love to hear what anyone else has to offer."

With a little coaxing from the other three, Joseph admitted that he had something. He rose from his seat, smoothed down the front of his clothes, and took a deep breath. Then with fire in his eye, he held out his arm and snapped into his recitation.

" 'Ay, tear her tattered ensign down!' "

The air was charged with energy as he stormed through the poem, pausing for a second at the beginning of each of the second and third stanzas. When he was finished, the others applauded and he sat down.

" 'Old Ironsides'!" exclaimed Emma. "What a stirring poem!" She turned to Lane. "And who's next?"

"I'd rather wait," he answered. "Though I run the risk of having a very hard act to follow."

"I was hoping to do the same," she said. "Wait for you and run the same risk."

"Oh, please, Emma," cried Cora. "Why don't you go next?"

"Oh, I suppose so. At least it will be over then." She stood in front of her chair. "Mine, also, is about a kind of a ship." She reached into her pocket and took out a folded piece of paper. "And I, too, must confess that I didn't get it perfectly by heart. I wrote it out, as a way of trying to commit it to memory, and if you'll permit me, I may have to glance at the script."

"What poem?" asked Joseph.

"The same author as yours," she answered, showing the sheet of paper. "I think you'll recognize 'The Chambered Nautilus.'" Then with a steady voice as she held the paper down by her side, she began.

"This is the ship of pearl, which, poets feign,
Sails the unshadowed main,—
The venturous bark that flings
On the sweet summer wind its purpled wings
In gulfs enchanted, where the Siren sings,
And coral reefs lie bare,
Where the cold sea-maids rise to sun their streaming hair."

Not until the fourth stanza did she have to look at her script, and one glance took her through to the end of the poem.

"Let each new temple, nobler than the last,
Shut thee from heaven with a dome more vast,
Till thou at length art free,
Leaving thine outgrown shell by life's unresting sea!"

An energetic applause followed her closing. "What a wonderful poem!" said Cora. "I know I read it in school, but I don't believe I ever really understood it until now. You read it so well. Would you lend me your copy?"

"Why, of course." Emma leaned forward and held out the sheet of paper, which Cora accepted by leaning also.

Lane looked away until she was sitting upright again. "If you're short on books," he said, "I'm sure I can find an extra copy of favorite poems to lend you."

"Oh, no," she said. "Don't bother. I've got books somewhere. They're just in the bottom of a box I haven't unpacked yet."

"Well enough."

Emma spoke up. "I think it's now time for Mr. Weller. Lane, will you favor us?"

"I really should have gone earlier. Yours was a much finer poem, with an unmatchable delivery."

"I did my little piece," she said. "Now our attention is all yours."

Lane's palms were moist, and he found himself smoothing out his shirt and jacket as he straightened up and took a breath. "Without further apology," he said, "I give you this." Looking first at Cora, he began.

"Helen, thy beauty is to me
Like those Nicean barks of yore,
That gently, o'er a perfumed sea,
The weary, way-worn wanderer bore
To his own native shore."

With the second stanza, he turned to Joseph and then Emma.

"On desperate seas long wont to roam,
Thy hyacinth hair, thy classic face,
Thy Naiad airs have brought me home
To the glory that was Greece
And the grandeur that was Rome."

Then with the third and final stanza, he returned to Cora.

"Lo! in yon brilliant window-niche
How statue-like I see thee stand!
The agate lamp within thy hand,
Ah! Psyche from the regions which
Are Holy Land!"

"Oh, how romantic!" exclaimed Emma as the applause died down. "Some of Poe's work leaves me cold, but I never tire of that poem."

"I think my presentation was the lightest fare of the day," Lane answered.

"Come, come," said Joseph. "You already said you weren't going to apologize. And so what if you didn't have time to memorize a pastoral elegy? And by the way, Emma, the lilacs in your dooryard are lovely."

"Aren't they, though? Everyone has praised them."

After a moment of silence, Emma spoke again. "Well, if any of you feel as worn out as I do by all of that exertion, I think it's time for cake and coffee."

Out came the blue willowware, as before, with pieces of cake similar in color to the pale cookies of the week previous. When everyone was seated, Joseph spoke.

"You all know the story of the Willow Pattern," he said.

"I don't," said Lane.

"Neither do I," Emma added.

Joseph looked around, and by his expression he seemed to take Cora's silence as a third declaration of the same kind. "It's actually rather well known," he began, "especially after Meredith's *The Egoist* and his main character, Sir Willoughby Patterne."

"Oh, my," said Emma. "I read that book, and I never hit upon it."

"It's a little allegory of true love," Joseph went on, "some of the details of which can be seen in the design." He tapped his fork on his plate. "As the story goes, there was a rich old man, in China, of course, who had a beautiful daughter. He wanted to marry her to a wealthy suitor who was close to his station in life. Here is the father's mansion, on the right. But the daughter had other ideas. She was in love with her father's secretary, and the two had declared their love in secret under the blossoming willow trees, which you can see here in the center of the pattern. The father, finding out about his daughter's wishes, locked her up in a pavilion in the garden, and said that when the peach tree was in blossom, she must marry the suitor he had chosen for her. At this point her true love rescued her and carried her away, over the Willow Bridge, right here. Eventually the gods turned them into birds, which you can see at the top of the design here."

"What a surprise," said Emma. "I had no idea there was a story connected with this pattern, though I knew the chinaware was very popular, of course."

Joseph pursed his mouth and then spoke. "Not

the first or last of its kind, I warrant, but a charming story all the same. And more uplifting than the one about the two lovers in Spain who plunged to their deaths on the rocks."

"Isn't it fascinating," said Cora, "to think about how much there is that a person does not yet know?"

Lane waved to Rox Barlow as he walked across the lobby toward the front door. The hotel proprietor, circumspect as always, nodded and then lowered his gaze to the newspaper he had spread out on the counter. Rox might wonder where Lane went every Thursday evening, but he had far too much repose to show any curiosity, especially to a long-term lodger.

When Lane arrived at the Apleys', the curtains were drawn as usual, so he couldn't see if anyone had arrived ahead of him. He knocked on the door and waited, then knocked again. The door opened to show Emma with a harried look on her face. She invited him in and stood aside.

"I'm afraid everything's up in the air. Joseph won't be here. Both he and Douglas had to go to a meeting. The schoolteacher left on short notice, it's not clear why, and they have to decide what to do about it."

"Left town?"

"Apparently so."

"That's too bad."

"Yes, it is. And I've got Trixie on my hands, and she's spitting up."

"Don't let me keep you—"

"Go ahead and sit down."

The baby's voice rose in a wail from beyond the kitchen, so Emma hurried away as Lane turned toward the seating area. The chairs had not been pulled around, and a clothes brush lay on the low table. He walked across the room to the chair he usually sat in, and after a few seconds of thought, he moved it into place. That should be enough. The two women could sit on the sofa.

He sat by himself in the dim room for a full ten minutes. The baby's voice rose and fell, then got louder as Emma came out to the kitchen. Lane heard the sounds of firewood being chunked into the stove and of water being poured into a basin.

A knock at the door gave him a start. Emma answered it right away, let Cora in, and gave her a quick summary of all the excitement. In conclusion she said that Trixie was doing more than spitting up and that she was going to have to give her a bath.

As Lane stood up to meet Cora, Emma withdrew into the kitchen and closed the door. Lane considered lighting a lamp, then decided to wait to see if Emma might come in to do it herself.

He turned to Cora, who was wearing a dark gray dress with full sleeves and a buttoned collar. She looked composed and in no hurry to sit down.

"I brought you something," he said, and reaching into the pocket of his evening coat, he brought out a small book.

Her eyes showed emotion as she took it in both

hands. "Why, thank you. Is this a page you have marked?" She put her finger on the little square of paper sticking out, and she opened to that page. " 'To Helen.' " She held it open long enough to read the first few lines, then closed it and gave him a tender look. "Thank you so much. I'll take good care of it."

"Do as you wish. It's yours to keep."

"Oh, I don't know if I could."

"Please do." They sat down, and he searched for something more to say. "Well, how have things been since our last time here?"

"Rather normal, I'd say. And you?"

"About the same. Work during the day, read a little in the evening. Not much more than that."

"It must be nice to have the time. To read."

"I suppose I take it for granted, but I've always had the habit."

She glanced at the book, which she had set on the table. "Well, I'm going to try to find time, at least a little."

"Poems are short. A few minutes now and then."

"It was very kind of you. And the poem 'To Helen' is special. I felt last time that you chose it for some reason."

"To tell the truth, I did. As I was looking for something to present, this one spoke out to me. Among other things, it reminded me that you were standing by the window the first time I saw you."

She gave a sigh, then said in a lowered voice, "But you saw soon enough that I wasn't any goddess."

"What do you mean?"

"Just a rough woman, with no refinement at all."

"Rough? I don't believe I've seen anything of that nature."

She was rubbing one hand over another. "Yes, rough. From the dishwater, and the wash water, and everything else I have to do."

"That's all honest work. And your hands can't be that bad. They look fine to me."

"That's because the light's so dim."

"Not at all. I've seen them in good light, and I've touched them. Here." He held out his right hand, and she gave him her left.

"See how they are?"

He rubbed his thumb across the back of her hand, and he moved the underside of his fingers against hers. He could feel a roughness, but it was nothing compared to the warmth that was flowing between the two hands. "It's not so bad," he said. "What kind of work do you do?"

"All the chores, and anything else that comes up."

"For example?"

"Why, just yesterday somebody had me help him unload a stack of lumber on a lot he invested in."

Lane winced. It seemed like heavy work for a man to put his wife to do, especially a pretty wife who didn't have as much ballast as some women did. But Lane held his tongue on that part and just said, "I think I know which wagonload that was. St. John had it shipped."

"I still haven't gotten all the splinters out," she said, turning her palm up but leaving her hand in his.

He leaned closer and stroked his left forefinger against hers until he felt resistance. "Here's one," he said. He bent closer and scratched with his fingernail, and her head came near his as if she was helping him watch. At the edge of his vision he saw her dark hair. He felt her soft breath and saw her lowered eyelids.

Then everything changed as the two of them, in the dim, closed room, met in a kiss. In the short moment that it lasted, he felt himself cut loose from everything as he fell into another world. At the same time that he was lost in the kiss, he had a clear awareness that he was doing something big, something he could never reverse or undo.

He opened his eyes and saw hers, close up, as they drew away from each other. He could tell it was no small moment for her, either.

They sat for another minute, her hand in his. He did not want this time to end, but he did not want it to be intruded upon, either.

"I suppose one of us should check on Emma," he said. "Or at least light a lamp. Could you imagine someone walking in on this dark room?"

"I'll go," she said.

Dusk had just begun to fall when he walked with her as far as her street. Lilac bushes were blooming in a couple of other yards they passed, and a row of red tulips stood like little soldiers in front of one house.

"Too bad things had to go to pieces on Emma,"

Lane remarked. "I think she felt bad about having to call off the event."

"Yes, poor thing. Though I don't know how much help Douglas would have been if he hadn't gone out."

"And poor Joseph, too. I'm sure he had something prepared, and now he'll be all pent up with it until next time."

She laughed. "And you? Did you have something ready?"

He gave her a sidelong glance. "I might have."

"I'm sure you did, and you won't tell me."

"I'll give you a hint. It was a sonnet."

"And you think I could guess which one, among thousands?"

"I would give you the first line, but in this case, I couldn't say the first without following through with the second."

"You like to tease me, don't you?"

"Perhaps because I think you like to be teased. But here it is.

"Shall I compare thee to a summer's day?
Thou art more lovely and more temperate."

"I wonder if you're still teasing me."

"Not anymore. And here's your street, where you go your way and I'll go mine." They stopped, and he took her hand. "All teasing aside, I want you to know that I have no regrets about that moment back there, but if you do, I will understand."

Her eyes were full of tenderness. "No, I don't at all. And even if I never saw you again, it would be a treasured memory."

"Well, I hope we do see each other again." He released her hand.

"So do I, Lane. Good night."

"Good night, Cora."

From there he floated to the main street, not noticing much at all as he played over the luscious scene in Emma's sitting room and then the parting with Cora. It seemed as if the perfume of the lilacs still hovered about him.

At the corner he turned right, thinking he might catch a glimpse of her at a cross street. As he passed St. John's office, dark now, and saw Joseph Saxton's store up ahead, he thought better of it. He turned around and headed back to the corner, where he saw two men loitering.

Just before crossing the street, he saw that one of them was Newt Collier and the other was a man named Quist, a slight, stoop-shouldered fellow who was given to standing on street corners and smoking his pipe, as he was doing now.

Lane crossed the street, nodded to the two of them, and went on his way to the Last Chance Saloon.

Chapter Three

Cora did not attend the next meeting of the literary society. Emma said only that she was busy at home. After a week of waiting to see her again, Lane felt let down, but he sat through the meeting with patience. Emma began the festivities with Bryant's "To a Waterfowl," a reverent piece, and Joseph followed with Browning's "Incident of the French Camp," in which the messenger boy falls dead after delivering the news of victory to Napoleon. Lane, whose spirits had not risen from the beginning of the meeting, chose not to recite the sonnet he had carried around in his mind for the past week. Instead, he reached into memory and brought out Gray's "Ode: On the Death of a Favorite Cat, Drowned in a Tub of Goldfishes."

Ringing a note of high moral seriousness, he directed the last stanza at Joseph:

"From hence, ye beauties, undeceived,
Know, one false step is ne'er retrieved,
And be with Caution bold.

Not all that tempts your wandering eyes
And heedless hearts, is lawful prize;
Nor all that glisters, gold."

When the light applause and laughter subsided, Emma said, "I don't believe I've ever heard, or read, that poem before. It's a rather odd one, it seems."

Joseph turned to her and intoned, "It's a cautionary tale. In order to make sense of the situation, of course, one needs to understand that the fishbowl was not of transparent glass but rather of some earthenware, such as crockery, so that in order to see the fishes, the cat has to be up on the lip. That's where she makes the false step. And, of course, the vessel has to be large enough to drown a cat." He relaxed his eyes as he turned them toward Lane. "You wouldn't mind giving us the first stanza again, would you?"

"Not at all.

" 'Twas on a lofty vase's side
Where China's gayest art had dyed
The azure flowers that blow;
Demurest of the tabby kind,
The pensive Selima, reclined,
Gazed on the lake below."

"There you have it," said Joseph. "I saw an illustration of the poem once, and the vase was indeed lofty—tall and narrow. But I think it could be tall and broad, just as well, as it is referred to as a tub in the title."

"Just as long as it's large enough to drown a cat," said Lane, catching himself at the brink of sounding too sharp.

"Exactly. It makes the tragedy."

Lane was back at his desk the next morning, casting a glance now and then toward the window, when he thought he recognized a dark blue shape as it passed out of view on the right. A moment later it reappeared, and he confirmed his recognition. Cora stood at the far edge of the window, her back to the office as she held her chin up and seemed to be looking out at the street.

Lane rose from his desk and walked out of the office. She turned to him as he faced her on the sidewalk.

"I'm sorry I missed things last night. How was it?"

"It was dreadful. Joseph was the lion. I think that if there had been a foursome, the balance would have been different. But at any rate, I missed your company."

"I wanted to be there, but I couldn't."

"Emma said you were busy at home."

She gave what looked like a submissive shrug. "Somebody left on a trip today, and I had to get his things together. Originally he wasn't going to leave until tomorrow, but he changed his mind and decided he wanted to leave today. So that changed my plans for yesterday evening."

"Too bad. But at least I get to see you now. Did he go on the trip to Newcastle?"

Her eyes widened. "Yes. How did you know?"

"I wrote the letters for it."

"Oh, of course." She looked down at the sidewalk and then at him again. Her eyes were blue as flax. "Well, I don't want to keep you from your work, but I thought I would let you know that if you wanted to talk for a few minutes this evening, I could manage to get away for a little while."

His heart raced. "Really? Where do you think we could meet?"

"I don't have that part figured out. I intend to go to Emma's, but just for a few minutes. I can stop someplace on the way back."

"Will your children be alone?"

"No, I've arranged with Mrs. Canby, the dressmaker, to come and sit with them for a while."

"That's handy."

"I just came from her place."

"Uh-huh. Well, let's see. What do you think about meeting in back of this building? I'll wait here, and then I can walk with you to your house, and we can talk then."

"At about eight?"

"Sure. It'll be getting dark then, so we won't attract so much attention."

"Fine. I'll look forward to it."

Their eyes met, and she turned away. He watched her for a couple of seconds, shapely dark blue, and then he went back into the office.

* * *

Lane waited as long as he could before leaving the hotel, and dusk had still not drawn in when he reached the back steps of the office. To make sure no one was inside, and to wear off some of his nervousness, he walked around the block. When he came back to his post, scarcely five minutes had elapsed.

Patience. He was the only person in town out of place, and if pressed for an explanation, he could say he came to listen to the night sounds and to get away from the confinement of his room. Cora would be here in a little while. She would be sitting in Emma's kitchen right now, having a pleasant chat and planning to leave. The person she called "somebody" would be somewhere at a way station between here and Newcastle, and St. John would be in his big house, perhaps reading a livestock journal as his wife tutored the girls on the piano. Virginia, the wife's name. No, that was the daughter, named for their noble state of origin. The wife was Victoria. And the other daughter was Elizabeth. Royal provenance for all.

Lane heard someone come out of the house across the alley, but a shed at the back of the property kept him from seeing anyone. That was just as well. Whoever it was would not see him.

The light was fading now. He saw movement and had to take a sharp look to identify a cat. Cora should be along pretty soon, unless something came up—one of the children took ill, or McGavin decided to come back for a handkerchief and start his trip over again tomorrow. He might be that kind. Drive around the block and check back in to see if the iceman was there, as in the joke back East.

Emma could keep a conversation going, he knew that, and if two women were talking by themselves, it might go on for a while. Cora might not be in a hurry to see him. For all he knew, she might be intending to tell him they had gone far enough. No, she didn't seem to have had that in mind.

Darkness had fallen now, and the moon was up. By his watch in the moonlight, it was well past eight, almost eight-thirty. If she didn't show by nine, he would go home—back to his room, where he could wonder if she came by a few minutes after he left.

When he looked at his watch again, the big hand had crossed the six. He closed the watch and sat with it in his hand, when all of a sudden he heard footsteps in the alley, coming from the right.

He stood up and tucked the watch into his pocket. The footsteps came closer, and then Cora materialized in the night.

"Hey," she said in a low voice.

He stepped close to her and took both her hands in his. "I was so afraid you wouldn't come."

"I got away a few minutes late, waiting for Mrs. Canby, and then I had to spend a respectable amount of time with Emma."

"Of course. I'm just glad you're here." He could see her eyes now, and they seemed to be drawing him close.

"I am, too," she said in a low breath.

They met in a kiss, which became a long, shifting series of kisses, followed by a close embrace. He kissed her on the neck below the ear, then brushed her hair aside and kissed her at the edge of her collar. Their lips met again. She was yielding in his arms now, he could feel it, the two of them standing in the darkness, shifting their feet to keep from tottering.

"No one saw you?" he asked as they drew apart. "No one followed you?"

"No, not at all. Not that I could see."

"How soon do you have to be back?"

"I can spend a few more minutes here."

"That's fine." He had his hands on her upper arms, near her shoulders.

"What's wrong? You seem nervous."

He thought he felt her trembling, but it might have been his own hands. "It's just that I feel so— out in the open here. Shall we go stand in the shadow of the back door?"

"Let's."

He led her by the hand and let her go up the step first, with his hand at her waist. Then he had her in his arms again, feeling her breasts against him as he clasped the small of her back. Their kiss lingered and shifted, and his hand moved to the back of her waist. She responded by pressing her full body against his. He kissed her neck again, and her cheek. He whispered in her ear.

"I've got a key. Should we go in?"

"Take me," she whispered. "Take me in."

He fumbled with the key, but in less than a minute they were inside, clinging again and locked in a kiss. Two stacks of burlap bags stood against the wall on his left, and the door leading to the storeroom lay on his right.

"Do you want to go into that room?" he asked.

"What's in there?"

"Just some old things. A deer head that used to hang on the wall up front, a couple of wobbly chairs, some old crates."

"This is fine here," she said. "I actually like the moonlight coming in through the front window."

"Let me get some of these," he said, moving to the bags, "and we can sit on the floor, where it's comfortable."

Her eyes in the moonlight, looking up to him from the burlap mattress they lay on, told him she had given herself to him all the way.

"It was unbelievable," he said, combing her loose hair with his fingers as he supported himself on his elbows, his midsection still pressed against hers. "It was more beautiful than I could have imagined. Even if we never saw each other again, this much would be perfect."

"Well, I certainly hope we do see one another again."

"Oh, yes, and soon, I hope."

As he walked her home, she said she would like to ask a question if he didn't mind. He told her to go ahead.

"I was wondering, and of course I'm in no position to ask, whether you have a girl somewhere. I can't imagine you not knowing someone, unless you've been recently disappointed."

He hesitated but did not slow his step. "Well, there has been a girl I've written to, but the feeling hasn't stayed very strong." He had an urge to tell her that the feeling had all but vanished since the moment he kissed her in Emma's sitting room, but he took the topic no further.

"Then I'm not causing you any trouble."

"No, not at all. To the contrary. But I hope I'm not causing you any."

"Not yet, anyway."

"If I do, or if you find yourself in trouble, just let me know, and I'll bow out if need be."

"I don't know if I'd want you to."

They were at her gate now, so they parted with a quick kiss in the moonlight. As he floated back to his room he had the presence of mind to keep an eye out, but he saw no one on the lookout. Inside the hotel, he crossed the lobby and gave a nod to Rox Barlow.

Lane was putting the finishing touches on a four-page letter. In the space at the bottom of the last page, he had drawn two long-stemmed flowers dancing with one another. Now with a set of wax crayons, he was coloring one flower red and the other blue.

He looked at the clock. He had half an hour yet until his meeting with Cora, and he could walk there in less than fifteen minutes. But in broad daylight, it wouldn't do to go there at the same time, so he would leave early. Even with most of the town listening to the traveling preacher, there might be some curious folks out on a Sunday stroll, and the fewer who saw anything at all, the better. He sealed the letter in an envelope, tucked it away in his jacket, twirled his hat, and sauntered out of his room.

Within ten minutes he reached the spot where the creek went around a yellow-ocher bluff. The red willows grew thick here, just as he remembered, and the branches were leafing out pale green. He found some sparse, mottled shade where the brush was highest, and there he waited.

Restlessness began to set in before one o'clock even arrived, and by a quarter past he was fidgeting. He wondered if he should have brought a book. No, he wouldn't have been able to concentrate.

He left the shelter of the willows and climbed up onto the creek bank. They had agreed to follow the bed of the creek, staying low, so as not to attract notice, but he hoped to get a glimpse of her. He saw nothing but the creek bottom itself.

Maybe something had happened. By some strange circumstance, McGavin had come home early, or Mrs. Canby had taken sick. For the hundredth time, Lane calculated the time that the husband had been gone. This was the third day; he would be on the farthest part of his journey. At the very quickest, he would just be starting back. Even with that assurance, Lane could not help imagining a scene in which McGavin on horseback caught up with his wife on foot and herded her back home.

One-twenty. Lane climbed the bank again, and this time he saw tan movement about a quarter of a mile away. He hurried back down and waited.

At last she arrived, stepping out of the brush and smiling. In an instant they were wrapped together, standing in the warm sun, pressing against one another. He tried to kiss her everywhere at once; her dark hair fell loose as she raised her head back and let him.

In the shade of the willows, composed now, with the first wave of their passion spent, they lay on the matted grass and spoke of small things. The talk came around to her husband. She expected him home tomorrow or the next day. Things would become more difficult then.

A heavy dread fell. "Do you think you'll still be able to see me, or even want to?"

"Of course," she said, with a soft smile. "We couldn't give this up, could we?"

They talked on, relaxed. She spoke of her early life, growing up on ranches where her father worked. She had met her husband when he came through working on the railroad. Yes, he was from Missouri. He went out and looked at land that the railroad would like to acquire. From there he became a speculator on his own. He liked to go to a place where things were moving, get what he could out of the middle, and move on. This was the third town they had jumped to in their eleven years together.

"But there's not much going on here."

"He sees something. There are other kinds of parcels that men can exploit, like rock quarries and gravel pits. He's done a couple of those. He wouldn't mind getting his hands on some coal or timber, but that takes more money than he's got."

"Is he working his way up to it?"

"Money seems to go through his hands pretty fast."

"Is he the kind that thinks he needs to make one big deal, and things will go swell from then on?"

She gave a look of mild surprise. "Yes, that's how he is."

"And he likes to make friends with men who move on that level. Men like my employer."

"Yes. It seems as if you know him pretty well."

"I haven't met him, but I know others like him."

Their conversation went on, returning to the topic of how little time they had and how much they wanted to be together. Cora said that whenever Somebody was about, she had to tend to him, and the rest of the time she had endless work around the house. Cooking, cleaning, heating water for baths, pressing clothes. She even had to haul in the coal and firewood, and haul out the ashes as well. It all added up with someone who liked to take three or four baths a week.

"Huh," said Lane. "Does that mean you have to go out by yourself sometimes, after dark?"

"As a matter of fact, I do. It seems to me we're starting to think in some of the same ways."

He smiled. "It seems pretty feasible, for one or

two times, at least. We probably don't want to establish any patterns."

"Yes. I could manage to run out of wood after he's settled into his bath with a glass of whiskey."

"And then we can do this," he said. As he drew near to her and closed his eyes, he saw her close hers.

Later, as they were tidying up their clothes and he was brushing off the back of her dress, he asked, "How will I know which night? Or does he have a routine?"

"No, he usually tells me on short notice. Like, before supper he'll say, 'I'll want a bath tonight.' " She lowered her voice as she imitated the original.

"Is there a place you can leave me a note, somewhere close by?"

She drew her brows tegether in a thoughtful expression. "How about under a rock? There are quite a few in the field there, not too far from the house."

"Why don't you do that? Pick a good-sized one, about thirty or forty yards from the back corner of your property?"

"That sounds like a good plan. Once we have a rock picked out, we can both leave messages there." She tugged down on the corners of her jacket. "Well, I have to be going."

"I hate to see you go, but I know you have to."

"It's so I can see you again." She tapped her finger on his nose.

"I like the way you think. But before you go, I don't want to forget to give you this." He reached into his jacket and brought out the letter.

Her eyes widened. "Thank you. I'll read it as soon as I get back."

Then she was gone through the willows and he was left alone, not like before, but calm and content. He lay on his back on the thick grass, gazing at the sky through the willow branches.

Far above, something moved in and out of his vision. He stood up and walked into the open, where he shaded his eyes and looked up. A hawk with broad, whitish wings was soaring above the plain. Trailing from its claws was a pale line, large enough to be a snake. A dark bird, too small to be a crow, was darting at the hawk, heckling it. The bird of prey sailed on, unruffled.

The rock sat by itself in the field, a gray lump the size of a small pillow. Lane knew it from all other rocks as soon as he saw it, and when he lifted it he saw grass underneath. Someone had moved it here. Sweet Cora. She wasn't afraid of a little work.

The second time he tipped it up, he found a white piece of folded paper lying on the grass. Somebody was going to have a bath tonight.

Lane waited in his room until the sun had set. Then he put on his hat and a traveling coat and walked out into the evening. Two blocks before he reached the edge of town, he detoured and took the lane that ran behind the houses and empty lots. McGavin's outbuildings were the last ones on the left, and he could loiter there in the dark. He came to the last cross street, glanced both ways, and moved along at his unhurried pace.

Halfway to the end of the lane where the outbuildings stood, he saw movement to his left. Looking across the empty lot, he saw Joseph Saxton on a dark horse, riding at a slow walk toward town and looking over the property on his left. His gaze went up and stayed for a couple of seconds, long enough for him to make an identification, and then he adjusted his reins and fixed his attention on the edge of the lot nearest him.

Lane did not have to wait long this time. As soon as it was dark, the back door opened and Cora came at a fast walk.

After their first long kiss, Lane said, "Of all people to see me, I was spotted by Joseph Saxton."

"Really? What was he doing?"

"It looked as if he was out riding around, looking at property. I hope he's not the type to make a peep."

"I don't think so. It seems to me that he tries to keep on good terms with everyone, being a merchant and all."

"Maybe so. I sense something from him, though—maybe it's more along the line of competition than actual antagonism."

"Oh, I think I know what you mean. Joseph wants a wife."

"What does that have to do with me?"

"He wants Emma, and me if I know any women, to help him find a wife. So he tries to show off in front of us."

"Well, I wish him the best."

She put her arms around his neck. "Let's not talk about him and use up what little time we have."

"You're right." A boldness came upon him, and he felt her hand on him.

Afterward, as they lay on his coat, she said, "There's the moon. Just like in your letter. Now each night I look out the window and think of us both looking at the same moon, like you said. It's a way of being together."

"I'm glad you liked what I wrote."

"It was lovely. And the two flowers—the 'darling buds of May.' I don't know how many times I read it and looked at that drawing."

He kissed her again, then propped himself up on one elbow. "I know you have to leave in another minute."

"I'm sorry."

"Don't be sorry. Let's not be sorry, either of us. But before you go, I need to tell you something. It's in this next letter I'm going to give you, but I want to tell you now, beneath the moon."

"Tell me."

"Cora, I love you."

"Oh, Lane, it makes me so happy to hear you say that. I love you, too. More than you could know." After another kiss, she sat up. "I really must go. I don't want to ruin things."

"I know," he said, rising to his feet and helping her up. "I have an idea. What would you think of standing by the window shortly after you go back in? That is, if everything is all right, and no one is in an uproar, you can stand there for a minute, and I'll take that as a signal."

"That sounds fine."

"It's like in a novel I read. Madame de Rênal hangs a white handkerchief in the dovecote, and her lover knows that everything has gone over all right."

"I'll do that, then, if the coast is clear."

Five minutes later, as he sat next to a clump of sagebrush across from her house, he saw the curtains draw back. Cora stood in the window, looking out and up. With a faint light in back of her, he saw but a shadowy form. She did not make any motion with her hand, and after a long moment she stepped back and closed the curtains.

Emma's living room did not seem to have changed, nor did Emma, as she sat on her end of the sofa and gave her visitors the news.

"Joseph is unable to join us once again, and he tells me he is afraid he does not have time to do these meetings justice. I don't know what either of you might think about whether to continue or not."

Lane looked at Cora and then at his hostess. "I was honored to be invited into the party to begin with, but if you think the original idea has run its course, I can go along with whatever seems the best way."

Emma nodded, then turned to Cora. "What do you think?"

"I don't feel that I've held up my part as it is. When I have been able to come, I've only listened. I haven't really contributed. I wish I had more time, and as you know, I love to read, but it seems as if there are only two of you now who are—well, who would be participating."

"That's not exactly how Douglas puts it, but as he says, on any given night there's likely to be one person indisposed, and with only three to begin with—"

"It's pretty understandable," said Lane. "I should say, reasonable. You've gone to a great deal of trouble, and at some point you have to decide how much the benefit is."

"I hate to think I'm turning you out."

"Not at all," said Cora. "My husband was hoping I could manage to get home earlier this evening anyway."

"Oh! I certainly didn't mean for anyone to leave so soon tonight. At the very least, we could have some coffee, and I did find time to bake some cookies."

The sky was still light when Lane and Cora bade Emma good night. When they were beyond earshot, Lane spoke first.

"Well, what do you think about Joseph? It seems as if he doesn't want to be a party to anything clandestine."

"It may be just as well. The less we see of his beady eyes, the better. But I still hold to my opinion that he is careful not to offend anyone."

"Let's hope so."

As they walked farther, she said, "I got your letter from under the rock. It was wonderful. I was touched by the part where you said you walk past my house every night."

"I thought you might have gotten it. I saw you at your window again last night."

"Yes. I decided I was going to try to stand there every night, for a few minutes at least, after dark. I know that each time I stand there, I give myself to you. Even if we can't be together all the time, we can be then. Like you said in the letter, it's like looking at the moon. We go outside of ourselves to a middle place, and meet there to be one."

"Yes, that's how I feel. Knowing that you're at the window, whether I can be there at that moment or not, helps me have faith that everything stays alive even in silence or separation." They walked for a moment without speaking until he resumed. "Do you think we could ever be together?"

With an earnest look she said, "I would like that."

Silence fell again until he brought up a new topic. "By the way, sometimes when I'm out at night, I feel that I have someone watching me."

"Oh, is it just a feeling, or do you see another person?"

"I see someone. A fellow named Newt Collier. Do you know who he is?"

"I've met him once. He's working on the house where we unloaded the lumber."

"Ah. Do you think he's some kind of a snitch as well? He sure seems to be on the watch."

"I don't know if he'd be keeping an eye out for someone else, but I know what you mean. The day I met him, he gave me a thorough going-over."

"Huh. What did what's-his-name think of that?"

"He's pretty sure of himself in situations of that nature, especially when he's got something over the other person, like money."

"Do you think he's ever had another woman?"

"Who?"

"Your husband."

She seemed to withdraw ever so little. "No, I don't think so. I think that if he did, I would know."

"I've heard other people say that when they were wrong. What do you think he would do if he found out about us?"

"Oh, I would be afraid for him to find out. I would not want to bring on his wrath."

"Against you? Has he ever been rough with you? Or are you afraid he might?"

"Oh, no, but I think he's capable of doing something to someone else."

"To me?"

"Well, yes, or anyone he thought had crossed the line."

Lane laughed. "Maybe I should warn Collier."

Back in his own part of town, Lane wondered if it was only his impression that his secret affair was no longer secret. Tom Sedley seemed to give him a knowing look in the Last Chance, as did Madeline Edgeworth when he met her on the stairs. Could be, could be. Maybe people were talking, and maybe they were just responding to what was written all over his face.

In his room, the words came to him plain and simple. He was in love. Regardless of what the woman might choose to do, he had to follow through with the way he felt. It would not be honorable to love one woman and continue to give expectations to another. It would not be fair to either. So he steeled himself and wrote a letter to Pennsylvania. After that, he wrote a letter to Cora, telling her that he was now free and unfettered, dedicated to their love and ready for the best.

CHAPTER FOUR

Lane's pulse quickened as always when he saw the white paper beneath the rock. He tucked it into his coat pocket and made haste back to his room, where he lit a lamp and scanned the handwriting that he had come to love. The first sentence made his heart sink.

Dearest Lane,

By the time you read this I will be gone, but only for a little while. I have received news that my father is not doing well back in Nebraska. I will be taking the train with the children, and you will be in my thoughts the whole time.

Please do not worry about not finding any letters under the rock for a while or that you won't see me at the window. I expect to be gone for about two weeks, and I will look up at the moon every night. My heart is yours.

As soon as I have returned, I will pass word to

you that I am back. Until then I will be, as always,

Yours in love,
Cora

Lane read the note several times, wishing there were more to it. She had put assurance in every paragraph, but as a whole, the letter did not have enough grist to sustain him in his emptiness.

Two weeks passed, then three, then four. Each day crawled by in the small, quiet world of Willow Springs. Lane did not leave town, for fear of missing a letter or getting it late. A couple of days after the fourth week had elapsed, St. John appeared at his desk one morning.

"Let's write a letter to McGavin. I think he's been fiddling around too long."

"Oh, really?"

"Yes. He's been gone for about a month. Said his wife's father had taken a bad turn. He was going to send her by herself, with the kids, and then he decided to go, too. He owes me for two wagonloads of lumber, which Collier has used up, and the building is stalled."

"What shall I put in the letter?"

"Something polite, to the effect that he should kindly note that each shipment was payable after thirty days, that I understand he may have other claims on his time, but that these matters are pending."

"Anything else?"

"That I wish him a safe journey back."

"Nothing about the house, then."

"No. It irritates me every time I see it, but my interest in the matter is limited to the lumber, so we'll keep it to that."

"Where shall I send it, or rather, address it?"

"I understand he's having his mail forwarded, so address it to him here in town, and when I sign it I'll take it to the postmaster."

"Very well."

Lane wrote the letter and typed it, then typed the envelope as well. Most of the time he found it easier to address the envelope by hand, but he thought he would rather not give a sample of his handwriting to McGavin. Also, on the chance that Cora might see the envelope, he would prefer not to give her cause for worry.

That evening, in the time between dinner and dark when the air was cooling, he went out on a walk. On the northeast edge of town he saw the half-built house. From what he could tell, Collier had not done a bad job. He had run the floorboards diagonally and had made neat cuts all the way along. Above the floor, the frame stood up stark against the evening sky. One gable end had been raised and tacked in place, with two planks sticking out in midair near the peak, to give the whole skeletal structure the look of a gallows.

From there, Lane meandered through town, turning every block or two, until he reached the southwest edge, where sat the house he had walked past so many times in the night. He saw no signs of life about it now—no human life, at least. A cottontail rabbit was nibbling weeds near the front step, and a magpie came soaring in from the north until it spotted a human and then veered away.

Ten more days passed. Summer had slipped into the latter half of July, hot and dry and dusty. From the edge of town, Lane could see the tawny rangeland stretch away in all directions. He wondered if Cora would come back, and if she didn't, how long he would stay in this town. This was supposed to be a dynamic time in a man's life, his early thirties, when he knew where he wanted to go with his life and was taking great steps to get there. But it was also a time when a fellow knew more, felt more, than he did when he was younger. It was a time when he could open up his life and share what he had to offer—ideas, comfort, stability. He didn't have to keep it all to himself; he felt he had grown into wanting to do for others.

He knew he loved Cora more than he could have a few years earlier. A corollary to that was his knowledge that he had more years behind him now, and hence fewer ahead. His awareness of time passing sharpened his sense of urgency, his desire to gather the rosebuds while he could. It also helped him realize he had more at stake now, that he was putting more on the line than he could have when his world was simpler and more self-directed. He had no idea what life would be like in a later part of the journey, but this part seemed like a dangerous one in which to take the plunge he had taken.

A full six weeks had elapsed when he received word from her. It came to him by the hand of Emma Apley, who stepped into the office one morning and handed him a sealed envelope with *Mr. Weller* written on the front in Cora's handwriting.

"Hello, Lane. It looks as if Cora is back at home. She asked me to give you this. She says she's busy trying to get caught up on everything, or she would drop by herself."

Lane took the letter, uplifted by the sight of the handwriting but revisited by the sinking sensation he had felt with her last letter. Emma did not act as if anything was out of the ordinary, so he smiled and thanked her. After she had walked out, it occurred to him that he could have said more, or inquired into the health of her family, or commented about the weather. But his apprehension had kept him nearly mute.

St. John was out of the office at the time, so Lane broke open the letter and read it with a quivering grasp.

Dearest Lane,

Finally I am back in town, after a trip that seemed to last forever. As you may know, at the last moment somebody decided to go along, and I could not find any convenient way to write you. I would not blame you if you have given up by now, but I have not.

I am going to try to find a way for us to meet. Look for a note from me, in the same place, in a couple of days. If the note is still there the next day, I will understand. It is my hope, however, that you want to see me as much as I want to see you, and that, before long, you will know again that I am, as always,

Yours in love,

Cora

That was good enough. The long wait was over. Just a short time now until he looked for the next letter.

Lane took his time eating dinner, then loitered in his room until dark. Anxious and hopeful, he went out into the night and took a roundabout route to the edge of town, pausing now and then to be sure he was alone. When he lifted the rock and saw the white paper, all worry flooded away. In place of the letter he left a folded piece of paper with a red rose he had drawn inside, with an inscription he had written: *Go, Lovely Rose, and tell her*. Back in his room, he read the message:

Dearest Lane,

I have spoken with Mrs. Canby, the dressmaker, and she has a good understanding as well as a soft heart. She has agreed to let us meet at her place. Her house is next to the vacant drayage business, I think you know where it is. If you tap at the back door shortly after dark tomorrow night, she will let you in.

I am more excited about this than I can tell you. May the hours fly between now and then.

Yours in love,

Cora

The hours did not fly. Lane had a fitful sleep, followed by a long, dreary day of accounts and correspondence. After dinner he felt on edge again, and he took a circuitous route to Mrs. Canby's, to wear away time and nervousness and to make sure he wasn't being followed.

Mrs. Canby opened the door and let him in with no time wasted. She led him through a dark washroom, into a dim hallway, and to a closed door. She opened it into a lamplit room.

"You'll be in here," she said, in a soft but high-pitched voice that he associated with buttermilk and corn bread.

Lane got a look at her now, a graying, middle-aged woman whose ample form was draped in a loose dress.

"Thank you." With his hat in his hand, he went into the room and sat on the edge of the bed. Then noticing that the door was ajar, he got up and closed it. He hung his hat on a nail and sat on the bed again.

He took in the room and its spare furnishings—a chair, a nightstand with a small candleholder next to the lamp, a wardrobe with one drawer. He understood that sometimes Mrs. Canby rented an extra room to workingmen, and this must be it.

About ten minutes later he heard voices in front, followed by footsteps in the hall. He was on his feet now, feeling his heart beat fast. The door opened, and Cora folded into his arms again.

"It's been so long," she whispered, after a long kiss. "I was afraid you had given up on me."

She felt somewhat like a stranger to him, and he knew they needed to tune up to one another again. "It was a long time, but I can't dismiss my feelings just like that."

"Oh, I missed you so much. When everything seems so crazy and full of turmoil, you're the one thing that makes sense."

"Did something happen to cause you to stay away so long? How is your father?"

"He's no better and no worse than he was. If all we had done was go to see him, we would have been back as planned."

"Well, what happened?"

"Oh, him!" she said, in a mixture of exasperation and disgust. "You never know what you're going to do that day. Most of the time we were there, I stayed with my parents at Cedar Canyon. And that was fine. My mother could use my help."

"And what did he do?"

"Oh, he would go into town for one thing or another. He's got a building there that he collects rent on, and a couple of property investments that he didn't finish all the work on, and he needed to take care of details in order to collect the last bit of money."

"What kind of details?"

"In one, it was getting the legal description straightened out, which required getting it surveyed again, moving a property line, and trips back and forth to the lawyer and the county clerk. The other was a matter of getting a clear title on some land that he had taken over from some people who just up and left. They had back taxes and who knows what-all. He filed a claim on it, and then supposedly he located someone and got a signature, but then the clerk needed a signature on something else, some kind of a quitclaim, and he was trying to see if there was a way around it. The people have disappeared, and I don't know where he even got the first signature."

"But he sold the property in the meanwhile."

"Oh, of course."

Lane shook his head. "Does he do things like that everywhere he goes?"

"Not exactly the same, but there's usually something unfinished."

"So he just strung things along, from one day to the next, while you were there?"

"Pretty much. I kept thinking we would leave, and then he would get up in the morning and say he had to go tend to this thing or that. I would ask when we were going back, and he would say, it depends on how much I get done today."

"Sounds like a quagmire. He left things hanging

here, too, you know. I had to write a letter for St. John."

"I thought you might have written it."

"Did he say anything?"

"Only that he'd gotten it. He tries not to show that anything is going to move him until he feels like it."

Lane frowned. "Do you like living like that?"

"It makes me crazy."

"I'll tell you, I don't do things that way. I meet my obligations, and I keep things tidied up."

"I know you do. And you find time to send me a Lovely Rose. What a difference! I was hard put to relax a single day I was gone."

"It surprised me that he went at all."

"He seemed to think I needed an escort. And then when we were there, he left me out at the ranch. If I did go into town, he kept me close by."

He tugged at her hands, which he had been holding all this time. "Let's sit down."

The two of them sat on the edge of the bed and met in another long kiss. When they drew apart, he said, "It was a long time, but now that we're together, it's as if that time is all swept away. In a sense, it's as if we had just stepped from one day to the next, but in another sense—"

"I know. But things are going to be better."

"You're still in tension. I can feel it. Do you want to live like this all the time?"

"Oh, Lane, I wish there were two of me. I'd run away with you tonight."

"But there's only one, and I don't know what you want."

"I want you. I want calmness and roses and some sense of order. I'm tired of lawsuits and debt collectors—"

"You can have me," he said. "I've got things cleared out in my life, and I can help you get a sense of order into yours." He shifted on the bed, and they reclined together. "So you tell me what you want."

Her eyes had gone soft in a subdued glaze, and her face had a relaxed, almost wounded expression. "I want you to understand me, which you do. And I want you to love me. Tonight and always."

For the first time they took off all their clothes together. She was not shy about her body, and as he lavished his love upon it, he had no doubt about their being back in tune with each other.

Later, as always, she was in a hurry to get herself together and be on her way.

"Always the question," he said, in good cheer now. "When may I see you again, my dear?"

"I don't have that planned yet."

"It would be good, for things in general, if we could plan for ourselves and not have to wait to respond to someone else's move. Don't you think?"

"Well, I can't go to the dressmaker's that often."

"Is there anything we could count on, not have to wonder when it might transpire, and not have to worry that it might get changed?"

She laughed. "He just about never goes to the outhouse."

"How so?"

"He does everything in the chamber pot, and I empty them every morning."

My God, she carries his slop like a servant. "Do you want me to meet you at dawn? I have an image of you like Hilda the milkmaid, carrying two pails in the morning dew."

She laughed. "Oh, no. We could meet at night. What I meant was, that's one place I can go by myself, and he doesn't interfere or want to sit in my lap."

"It sounds like something I could manage, that kind of meeting."

"What do you say, then? Two nights from now? At about nine? Something we can count on."

"That sounds fine."

He was sitting on the edge of the bed as she buttoned the front of her blouse. He pulled her to him and kissed her breast through the fabric. She leaned into him and then straightened up to finish buttoning.

"Do you think you could stand at the window tonight, provided that you get back without any trouble?"

She pushed her bust forward. "Like this?"

"Any way you want," he said, "just so that you don't attract too much attention inside."

"Like Helen, then."

"Yes. All a beautiful woman has to do is be present."

"I don't know how beautiful I am, but I can do that much."

After she had been gone a few minutes, Lane left two silver dollars next to the lamp on the nightstand. Then he went out, thanking Mrs. Canby on the way. He felt calm and relaxed in the cool night, and he walked without worry. Outside Cora's house he waited but a few minutes until the curtains parted and she appeared. She put her hands on her hips, looked from one side to another, and squared her shoulders. When she stepped back and drew the curtains, he went on his way.

Drinking a cold mug of beer in the Last Chance Saloon, he felt the relaxation settling in. Their long moment together lingered with him, perfect and rounded. Her appearance at the window gave their meeting an assuring close, a sense of safety as if the whole experience were a stone dropped into a pond. He could see it settling to the bottom, next to others, safe like a jewel.

Lane sat at his desk, transferring figures into the ledgers. It gave him a small satisfaction to see that St. John had gotten payment for the lumber, but he also took pleasure in knowing anything to McGavin's discredit. From Cora's comments, it seemed as if he had the habit of keeping other people tied up in uncertainty and that he tended to foul his nest before he moved on. As for the way he treated his wife, a fellow could feel justified in treating her better, and from a practical point of view, the better that others might get to know McGavin, the more they might sympathize with his wife if she tried to make a move.

The door opened, and a jolt of surprise went through him as Cora walked in. She was wearing a cream-colored dress with dark brown trim. Her hair was pinned up, her face had a flush of color, and she was smiling.

"Well, hello," he said. "What fair wind brings you here?"

"The cat's away."

"Oh, really?"

"Yes, he went somewhere with your employer, so I knew the coast was clear."

"He went with St. John to look at the breeding stock?"

"Yes. He had me press a good shirt for him, and he got scrubbed up to look his best. I think he expects to meet some influential men at the event."

"There might be some there. Does he fancy himself a cattleman?"

"He'd like to move in those circles, I think. I hear him talking of late about this breed and that, good traits, weight gain—as if he wants to practice the language."

"Good for him. Maybe he can join the Cheyenne Club and spend half the winter there." He met her eyes, which were steady and gray. "So what are you doing right now? Running errands?"

"Oh," she said, turning on one foot. "Since I knew you had the office to yourself, I thought we might be able to move tonight's meeting up a few hours. Somebody might get home late enough to complicate things, and here we've got four walls."

Lane glanced around at the openness of the front office. "Here?"

She smiled and frowned at the same time. "Not right here. But if I remember correctly, there was a room in back, with a deer head you didn't show me."

"It was dark."

"But you know how it is, to have your curiosity raised and then to be kept in suspense."

He rose from his chair. "No reason you should have to wait now. It's actually a doctor's office, but fortunately, the doctor is in."

That afternoon it rained, and the storm was just clearing away when he locked the office. He decided to take a stroll, so he walked out to the east edge of town, away from any of the places he haunted, and took in the freshness. The rain had settled the dust, but the smell of parched grass, now damp, hung in the air. From somewhere nearby came the silver song of the meadowlark. Lane set his hat back on his head and took a deep breath. Casting his gaze around to the vast country, he saw the pine ridge several miles to the north, its dark trees spotting the dry prairie. Beyond that, a blue sky stretched forever. The fluting of the lark sounded again. There was something to admire in this country, in spite of the desolation.

* * *

Lane raised his head at the sound of the front door latch, and his stomach lurched as the door opened and McGavin stepped in. The man did not speak to him, as if it were more befitting him to snub the secretary, but rather glared at him as he walked past and into St. John's office. Lane noted that McGavin was a big man, above average in height, meaty-faced and starting to spread at the girth. Walked like the bull of the woods. If he knew how much nerve his wife had, or where she had been at this time yesterday, it might take some of the swagger out of him.

After a short conference, McGavin walked out, still not deigning to acknowledge the man at the desk. Just as well. If the man wanted to think someone else didn't exist until he chose to recognize the person, that was his lookout.

Lane opened the letter in his room. At first glance he wished it were longer, but as he read it his apprehension faded.

Dearest Lane,

I wish we had time for a visit to the doctor's office, but I am doing what I can right now. Emma has a little event planned for tomorrow evening, Tuesday, for some of us to meet the new schoolteacher. She is from Illinois and will be staying with the Apleys. I expect to go to Emma's around seven, after I have gotten supper for everyone here. I won't stay long. When I leave I will go up

to the main street and then back around home that way. If it is convenient for us to cross paths, we can talk for a little while at least. I will look for a better opportunity soon. Meanwhile I remain
Yours in love,
Cora

At a little after seven, Lane walked out into the evening. A coolness in the air told him fall was not far away, and he wondered if the shorter days would bring more opportunity or if the colder weather would bring loss. He wondered if he could go on like this through the fall and winter. He could push for a change, but then he might end up with less than he had now. Fear of that prospect dragged on him, and he brushed away the thought.

He walked the streets, confident that the residents of Willow Springs were used to his haphazard movements by now. He went north and south a couple of times, then east and west, always on the lookout for Cora, until he saw her halfway between Emma's house and the main street. He whistled, and when she turned she waved.

He caught up with her in a minute. "Well, how was the meeting?"

"Oh, very nice. Her name is Frances, and she is from Illinois."

"Were you all women there?"

"No. Joseph was there—still is, in fact—and so was Douglas, of course."

"I see." They walked on for a few steps until he said, "Anything new?"

"Not that I can think of. And yourself?"

"No, nothing new. Just living from day to day, doing my work, waiting to see if things are going to go anywhere."

"I'm sorry," she said. "I know things have been difficult since I got back. Somebody's been in a bad mood just about all the time, and that gets passed on to me. If I think I want to go somewhere, he'll say, 'Why don't you just stay home?' " She lowered her voice as she did when she imitated her husband.

"And you just go along with everything."

"I don't know how to do things any different."

"When he's away, you've got plenty of initiative. But that changes when he's around."

"I guess you're right."

"Do you think things are going to change?"

"They can't go on like this forever."

"That's for certain, but they aren't going to change by themselves, either. It's not likely that he'll step out in front of a train."

She gave a nervous laugh. "I know."

They turned right on the main street and headed west.

"You know," he said, "I've been thinking that what I need is a little time away. I think I could get it."

She looked at him in surprise. "And what would you do?"

"I've been thinking of going to Chicago."

"To stay?"

"No, just to see things. You know, they've got that big exposition going on. All sorts of modern things to see. They've built a whole city for it, with exhibit halls as big as this town."

"And you'd like to go see some of it."

"Yes, as much as I could. Of course, I'd rather see something like that with you, but—"

"Oh, I'd love that." She cast her eyes down. "But you can't wait for me. It might be weeks, or even months, before we could do something like that together."

"Well, this thing is going to go on for a few months. Through October, I think. I just started thinking about it recently, and I could ask for some time when things slow down, which is about then."

"I don't want to keep you from doing something you want to do."

"I'm not going to do it right away, if I do it at all, and if there's a chance we might be able to see it together, I would be willing to wait to see if we could."

They had a block to go until she would have to turn right toward her house. "We've had a lot of good times together," he said. "I'd be hard put to say which has been the best—under the open sky, or within four walls, as you say."

"It's all been perfect."

"Yes, it has been, except it always has to come to an end."

"I know."

"Even a walk like this is fine with me, but I need some assurance that sooner or later you're going to get out from under the thumb of Mr. McGovern."

She laughed. "That's a good name for him."

"One among many. But as I said, I'm willing to wait awhile if I think there's a prospect for change."

She gave him a sincere look. "There is."

"And in the meanwhile?"

"I'll find every chance I can to let you do what you did the other night, at Mrs. Canby's."

"Or even a portion of it, as in the doctor's office."

"It was good for my pulse."

He took a deep breath. "Mine, too. But here's your corner."

Without touching, she went on her way and he went on his, back to the hotel.

Chapter Five

Lane stood at the edge of the street, hearing the wind whistle through the open rafters. Collier had the frame of the roof in place, with the lateral strips ready for the shingles. Two stacks of lumber, battens and boards for the siding, stood at the ready. At a glance, Lane could account for the three invoices he had logged so far, all of them through St. John's lumber interest in Newcastle. The shingles would be forthcoming. From the looks of things, Collier was going to have to make good time if he hoped to avoid frosty mornings on the roof slats. Lane hunched into his coat and continued his walk.

On the north edge of town, he looked out over the range. Clouds had piled up in the northwest—dark, heavy clouds in layers like folds of felt. The wind coming out of that corner brought the smell of rain. Lane put his back to the weather and headed for the shelter of his room.

Seven o'clock and night falling. A patter of rain

on the window. In a little while it would be time to put on his hat and coat and go out to look for a letter. It might be a bath night, but he would not know until he got a message. She was supposed to leave word, one way or the other.

When he lifted the rock, which was cold and wet, he found nothing but dry grass underneath. He patted it to make sure. Rain was slanting down, and as he had not thought to bring gloves, the rain and the rock chilled his hands. He thrust them into his coat pockets and stood with his back to the storm.

It was his fault. He left the room too soon. If he went back right away, she might come skipping out and he would miss everything. He could walk to the hotel and back, but he would get just as wet as he would if he kept his post for a while.

Ten minutes stretched into twenty, and then he didn't try to read his watch anymore. He walked out through the sagebrush and came around in front of the house, where all was dark. Crossing to the empty lot and coming through the alley to the outbuildings, he saw that the back of the house lay in darkness as well.

By now he was starting to shiver, so he picked up a brisk pace to go back to his lodgings. A few yards before he reached the cross street, he heard hoofbeats crunching on the wet road. A closed carriage crossed in front of him. He did not recognize the driver, wrapped in an oilskin slicker, nor did he recognize the coach. Whoever was inside was traveling in relative comfort and probably not hiding from anyone.

As for himself, he was wet and cold and dejected, a lurker in the rain now skulking back to his den. The thought of where Cora might be at the moment did not raise his spirits at all.

In his room once again, he changed into dry clothes and was able to build up his body heat, but he could not shake off the dreariness he felt at being such an outsider. Silence and not knowing made for unending worry as he sat in his chair, too dispirited even to read. At a little after ten he crawled into bed, but sleep was a long way off.

He tried to focus on the times when things had gone well—sunny afternoons, moonlit nights—but the cold, wet darkness kept coming back. He summoned up wisdom he had come across in his reading and had stored away—how the greatness of this kind of passion came from overcoming difficulties and uncertainties, how courage proved itself when a man had to face danger alone—but the ideas gave him little comfort. He was not the hero of a French novel, having intrigues for the sake of adventure, and besides, in those stories, the affairs always ended with flamboyant disaster.

Maybe this one would end in such a way. He imagined scenarios in which the adversary walked in through the front door and shot him point-blank at his desk; or dark riders plucked him off the street and took him to a distant cottonwood, where he would twist in the air until some sheepherder found him. Fancy thoughts. In real life, he just languished from hour to hour, day to day, not knowing where things would go.

At daybreak he got up, having slept very little, and put himself together for a day at work. Downstairs at breakfast he saw the day outside, heavy clouds and a light drizzle. He wore the same hat and coat as the night before, thinking they could dry out at the office just as well as in his room.

When St. John came in at nine and put his own hat and coat on the rack, he seemed to take note of the damper items. If he did, he said nothing.

The gloom did not lift all morning, neither outside nor in. After the dinner hour, St. John said it was too early in the year to start up the coal-burning stove but it wouldn't be a bad day to burn papers. He told Lane to bring out a stack from the storeroom. Lane went to the back of the building, patted his hand on the nearest pile of burlap, and went into the closed room. In the corner, below and to the left of the deer head, sat half a dozen stacks of paper—old bills and notices and insignificant bits of correspondence stored away in the warm months for burning in the other half of the year. He picked up a stack and carried it out front, where he fed it, a few sheets at a time, into the stove. If the fire did not warm the room much, at least it gave a blaze and the suggestion of heat.

When the workday came to a close, Lane, having no place else to go and with his energy at low ebb, walked back to the hotel and climbed the stairs to his room. He turned the key, opened the door, and stopped short. On the floor in front of him lay a white envelope with his name written on it. The handwriting made his pulse jump, almost as much as if Cora had been sitting in his chair.

How the letter arrived there, he could not be sure. Mail that came for him at the hotel was usually put in his pigeonhole at the desk, then handed over without the slightest expression on the part of Rox Barlow. Sweet Cora. She knew what he needed. She wasn't going to make him wait till dark to find something under the rock, and she had found a way to bypass the front desk. She could be plucky.

Smiling now, with his door closed, he broke open the letter.

Dearest Lane,

I am so sorry about last night. If I could have gotten out, I would have. The good news is that I can meet you at Mrs. Canby's tonight, at a little after dark. I have to be quick right now. I am sending this by her, and I trust that you will get it all right. Until later, I am

Yours in love,

Cora

Lane read the letter a second and a third time. Everything was fine. He would have her in his arms again, that very night, in the best of ways.

From his seat on the edge of the bed he heard voices at the front door, then footsteps in the hall, and the click of a doorknob. The door opened and Cora walked in, calm as a sailboat on a clear day.

She wore a dark blue jacket and a matching skirt, with a white blouse buttoned almost to her chin. The buttons were round and shiny, dark blue shading to purple, like an apothecary's bottle.

He had his arms around her waist, pressing her to him, as he covered her face and neck with kisses. "Darling. My darling."

"Say my name," she whispered.

"Cora. My darling Cora. I love you. Love you, love you, my dear Cora."

He tugged at one of the buttons with his teeth, and she arched her back into him. He undressed her, piece by piece, not rushing it but not wasting any time, laying each garment in a neat pile on the chair. He lifted her in his arms and stowed her beneath the covers; after the work of another moment, he joined her.

Slow, he told himself. *Slow.* He wanted to do everything at once, his lips running all over her. *Slow.* He started at the ankle, kissed the hollow spot beside the bone, caressed the two sides of her thigh with his fingertips. Kissed her smooth calf, then the underside of her knee.

Afterward, as he lay on top of her and ran his fingers through her dark hair, he saw that look in her eyes that said she was all his, at least for this time together.

"Cora," he said. "My beautiful Cora. I don't see how we can be apart. I ask myself that basic question, and I come up with the same answer, over and over. We were meant for each other. We have to be together. Do you see how it could be any other way?"

Her eyes were blue now, almost as dark as the buttons he had seen on her blouse. "No, Lane, I don't."

"When I think of it in absolute terms, that's the answer I get. As if it were destiny."

"I believe that."

He rolled over onto his side, with his hand on her hip. "Sometimes I despair, but I have that to cling to."

"I'm sorry," she said, moving her head back and forth.

A pang of fear. "Sorry for—?"

"For last night. I couldn't find a moment's privacy to write a note, much less go out to leave one."

"I waited for a while, hoping you might step out at least for a moment."

"Did you wait long?"

"I don't know. Maybe half an hour. Long enough to get wet and cold, to the skin."

"I'm sorry."

"Well, it's no one's fault but my own. I'm the one who stood out there. I was expecting something, one way or the other, but eventually I figured out that nothing was going to happen."

"I'm sorry."

"You've said that enough times, I think. But I don't mind knowing what did happen, if it's something you can tell me."

"Well, there's not much to tell. Somebody got to drinking his whiskey, and when he starts in on it early, he doesn't care for a bath or anything like that. Doesn't even care to wash his face."

"Even if you didn't go out for firewood, couldn't you have gone out for some other reason?"

"He said the weather was too bad for anyone to go anywhere."

"You mean, he even tells you where to piddle?"

"He was not in a good mood, and I didn't want to cross him. So I pressed clothes and listened as he went on and on."

"So you did have firewood, if you heated your irons."

"Yes. He had me bring some in earlier."

"He's got a lot of moves. Living up to the name of McGovern."

She gave what seemed like a forced laugh. "All of that."

"I think he's onto us and doesn't want to show it, as if by recognizing it he would give it some—I don't know—validity, or existence. But if he refuses to recognize it, then he can bully it. Make you try to keep it hidden, make you keep it at the level of something to lie about."

"I don't know."

"But you say he's getting surly."

"He's always been surly. Just more so of late."

"If he's got something eatin' on him, what else would it be?"

"I don't know. It could be anything."

"I gather that he was on some kind of a harangue last night."

"He was. But he didn't touch on anything that close. He went on and on about Emma."

"Emma? She seems rather unoffending to me."

"She is. But he says he doesn't like me spending that much time with her. As if I did. I told him she was busy with the new schoolteacher, that Frances was her new friend and we didn't see each other that much."

"That's how it seems to me."

"Apparently not to him. He went on about how he didn't like the ideas I came home with when I did go to her house."

"What ideas?"

"Oh, I made the foolish mistake of telling him about 'The Chambered Nautilus' and how it inspired a person to think about growing into a newer self. He laughed at me at the time, but when he threw it back in my face later, it had grown into a whole set of ideas, all acquired from the company I kept at Emma's—as if I wouldn't have ever had a thought of my own."

"Dangerous ideas, to him."

"He says that the ideas I picked up at Emma's have made me not pay enough attention to what I should be doing at home."

"Like waiting on him, hand and foot."

She didn't answer for a moment. Then she said, "Anyway, I just found out from Emma yesterday that he had a talk with Douglas. Told him he was glad our little get-togethers had come to an end, that nothing good seemed to come of them, and that Emma and I are not good influences on one another."

Lane's pulse took an angry jump. "He's got quite a bit of cheek, this fellow."

"That's the way he is. The result of it is that Emma feels like she's in hot water. She doesn't know if Douglas told someone about the letter she delivered, but she made a point of telling me that she didn't care to deliver any more."

"I can't blame her for that. Do you think she's got some idea about you and me?"

"I think she might, though I haven't told her anything. And I think she might even be envious. Douglas keeps a pretty tight rein over her house, and she has told me on a few occasions how exasperated she gets. But she doesn't want any trouble."

"In essence, then, he's bullying both of you."

She gave a half shrug as she lay with her head on the pillow. "I guess so."

Lane exhaled, long and slow. "I don't know about someone having that much to say about what you think and who you see. I should say, *whom* you see."

"Well, that's the way he is."

"He seems just a bit intrusive, and I still think he's onto something, as if he doesn't want to recognize A, so he puts it all in terms of B."

"I don't know."

"By the way, what do you do with the things I've written you? He strikes me as the type that would go through things like that."

"I have them all inside a pillow slip, beneath my underthings in a dresser that I have to myself."

"You think they're safe? You must have a pretty good-sized bundle by now."

She smiled. "You've written some wonderful

things, and drawn some lovely pictures, and I've kept every bit."

"And you're not afraid of any of it falling into his hands?"

"No. He doesn't go through my things."

"Well, I'd say you can't be too careful. What would you think of giving them to me, for safekeeping?"

Her eyes went soft. "Do you want me to tell you the truth?"

"Of course."

"I'm afraid that someday I won't be able to see you anymore, and at least this way I'll always have some of you."

"That's a nice thought. But if you wanted to, you could think of it the other way, that instead of not seeing me at all, you could fix things so you could see me all day every day."

"I'd like that," she said, putting her hand on his waist.

"But that means you'd have to do something about this fellow McGovern."

"I know. But don't you think we've talked about him enough tonight? Let's not waste what little time we have together."

She shifted, and as he found her breast she put her hand on the back of his head.

"To hell with McGee," he said, moving from one breast to another and pressing his fingernails into her buttock. As he felt her respond, he told himself that these moments would prevail, come what may.

* * *

Lane walked alone on the rangeland north of town, glancing from time to time at the pine ridge in the distance and wondering what the country looked like on the other side. People called it the breaks, and it was supposed to be a good place for deer. It also had a reputation for winter weather, when snowstorms hovered there.

For right now, the sky was blue. The clammy weather of the last couple of days had cleared out, and first frost would come along before many more days had passed. At the moment, though, the sun was warm on his back and cast a clear shadow on the grass.

The golden moments of the night before came back to him, just as he had told himself they should. Summon up the scene as he might, though, he could not overcome the persistent knowledge that he was something to be lied about and kept in the dark. McGovern had to know; he couldn't be that stupid. Rather, on some level he chose not to recognize it, and by doing so he might be a pretty good manipulator. By keeping things from coming out in the open, he abetted their remaining a lie, and by doing that, he defined the thing that his wife could not utter.

Lane shook his head. It made him dizzy to think in circles, to interpret how a man could take pleasure in making a woman cheapen herself by his definition. At one point, much earlier, Lane had thought that a man who seemed to care so little for his wife might not mind being separated from her, but now he could see that McGee had far too strong an attachment to his chattels. Governing a grown woman—telling her when and where she could piddle, as if she were a house dog—must be a pleasure he would not want to give up.

As for himself, loitering near an outhouse with the hopes that his true love might sneak away from her jailer and come out to tell him whether she could see him, he did not feel very proud. He was so far from walking hand in hand with her in broad daylight that he saw himself as a kind of captive as well, at one remove. He fancied for a moment that an observer was up on the pine ridge, looking down at him, a manacled figure. That was dreary enough, but drearier still was his awareness of how normal it had seemed to him to be lurking there, and how normal it seemed to her to want to sneak out and to be kept from doing so.

He pictured himself again as seen from the top of the ridge, a lone wanderer on the landscape. He had heard of men who wandered out into the winter plains or summer deserts, into mazes of canyons, buttes, and mesas, never to be heard of again. The immensity of it all was alluring, so much better than, as they said, dying in the street. But he knew he was not going to do either—not very soon, at least. Absurd as things sometimes seemed, he was going to go back and see them through.

He was about to take a seat in the dining room when Madeline Edgeworth spoke to him from the next table.

"You're welcome to sit here if you'd like. I wouldn't mind the company."

Lane paused with his hand on the back of the chair and raised his head. Madeline had a congenial expression on her face, no hint of the dark temptress who would drive apprentices to rob their masters and murder their uncles. Lane smiled at the reasonable idea of sitting at dinner with a fellow lodger.

"Thank you," he said. "I would enjoy the company as well."

He sat in the chair opposite her as his roving glance took in her dark eyes, dark hair, and full bosom. She was not a mysterious woman to him, just distant, or, as he thought of her now, independent. He knew she lived on her own means, some of which came from acquired earnings, but he didn't know the names of any of the men she kept company with. He doubted that St. John would be among them, but he knew she didn't have to work out of a saloon or go along with any old freighter who came along. She could pick her company, and for dinner she had picked him.

They breezed through the topics of health and weather, in and around ordering the evening special as usual. Madeline pulled the edge of her napkin through thumb and forefinger before she shook the cloth and laid it in her lap.

"There's probably enough time, before the bad weather sets in, to go on a trip."

"Probably so," he agreed. "Are you thinking of going somewhere?"

"No. It was just an idea." She took on a shrewd look and said, "How about you?"

"No," he said, looking down at his own napkin. "I've got no desire to go anywhere right now."

"Glued to the spot, aren't you?"

"Huh?" He looked up.

Her face softened. "You can take this for what it's worth, Mr. Lane Weller. But I like you. You're a nice man, always polite, always minding your own business, not looking to bother anyone."

"I try."

"I may or may not have seen more of the world than you have. Unless I miss my guess, I'm a year or two older than you at the most."

He shrugged. "Probably pretty close."

"But sometimes, a person on the outside can see things that someone on the inside can't, for reason of being up too close."

"The forest and the trees."

"Something like that, but also like the hand in front of your face." She held up her right hand spread out flat, with the palm against her nose.

"I think I follow you."

"I've got no reason to be telling you this, except that I like you and wouldn't want to see you go through a lot of misery."

"Is it that obvious?"

"It's written all over you, Mr. Lane Weller."

"Just call me Lane, is fine."

"All right. But as I said, yes, it is obvious. About half the time you mope around with a lost look on your face, and if I hadn't seen it on my own I probably wouldn't care."

"Uh-huh. And you think it's apparent to others as well?" He wondered if lately Rox Barlow had made more effort than usual to act discreet.

"Anyone who cares to look. This town isn't much bigger than a fish tank. At the very least, some people can tell what's going on. Most of them probably don't care how you're going to come out of it."

"I appreciate those who do."

"I know what it's like to wait for someone who never showed up."

That stopped him. "And you see me headed for the same thing."

"I think you're setting yourself up for a big disappointment sooner or later, and if it's much later, I think you're throwing yourself away in the meanwhile. There. That's the advice from your dear aunt Em. Unasked for, and free of charge. You could go to Tom Sedley, and he would tell you the same thing."

Lane's first thought was that Tom and Madeline had been talking about him, as Tom was the only other person to whom he had mentioned the Chicago fair. His second thought was that he might have two friends at a time when he wasn't sure he had any. "Thanks," he said. "I appreciate it. But I'll probably go on being a fool for a little while longer."

She smiled. "I have no doubt. And like they say,

if two convince a fool against his will, the fool will have his own opinion still."

"Oh, yes. And there's no fool like an old fool."

"You're not that old, Lane, but you will be if you don't look out for yourself. No one else will."

"So you think I ought to take a trip somewhere."

"That's just one idea out of several. But you'd be taking care of yourself. Like I just said, no one else will."

"Well, thanks for the impression. It does seem as if you're taking some trouble to look out for me."

"As I mentioned earlier, I like you and I hate to see you suffer. But if it comes right down to it, it's me first." She gave a pretty smile. "Because no one else is going to put me there."

Lane hesitated. He was sure he put Cora first, at least part of the time, but he knew she didn't put him there. Nor did McGee put her there. "I can't disagree with anything you've said."

Her bosom rose as she straightened in her seat to make way for her plate. She smiled again and said, "Even if you did, there would be no harm."

After dinner, as they were having a cup of coffee, Lane saw a man on the sidewalk turn and look in through the window. It was Quist, the stoop-shouldered one, turning in the stiff manner he had. A moment later, the man entered the dining room and sat at a corner table, where he picked up a newspaper and held it aloft. With his left side to the rest of the room, he puffed on his pipe and turned the pages.

"How about that fellow?" said Lane. "I get the feeling that he keeps an eye on me."

"You, too? I think he keeps both eyes on me. But it won't do him any good."

Cora's letter said *Look for me around seven*. She planned to run out of wood after supper. They could meet at the woodshed, and now with their understanding, Lane was never expected to wait more than half an hour. He had told her he could do that standing on his head, but with the weather turning as cold as it had, he was content to stay huddled in his hat, coat, and gloves. He saw light in the window and imagined Cora tending to her family inside.

What did Cora put first? She didn't talk much about her children, probably because they constituted such a tie to her husband, but he knew they took up the center of her life. Sometimes, she said, McGee came crowding in as number one, but most of the time she managed to keep her children there. That left her at number three, and by Lane's calculation, it put him at number four on his best days. He wondered if some days he had a number at all.

What he needed was more of Madeline Edgeworth's philosophy, "If it comes right down to it, it's me first." If he was better at that, he wouldn't have to worry about what number he was on somebody else's scale.

There was no arguing with the children being most important. Every mother he had heard on the subject made a point of saying the kids came first. But they were odd things to think of sometimes. Little creatures that spit up white curds and squirted out brown pools, then grew up to spy on their parents. Cora said that little Franklin, now ten, had been taught to tell his papa whenever Mama was gone for very long. Little Belinda would be next. Maybe McGovern would send her out on detail when Mama went to the outhouse.

Enough of the unkind thoughts. Cora had her children, and there was no touching that.

He had been standing for a good fifteen minutes when the back door opened and she came scurrying out in a heavy woolen overcoat.

"How are things?" he asked as he touched her gloved hands with his.

"I've got him in the bathtub, and I need to get back before long to put in some hot water."

For a fleeting moment, he had an image of the man at his most vulnerable. A shot in the head would do it.

Of course it wouldn't, with little Franklin and Belinda close at hand, and the rest of his own life a disgrace. But it was an amusing thought, like burning down the house that Collier was building. Just an idea, all in sport.

"Is there any room in the shed?"

"Yes, a little. I think it's better than out here, but it'll be cold no matter what."

Urgent kisses, fumbling and hurrying, and the good deed done. He lay against her, his warmth to hers.

"Do you have a minute to hear something I've had on my mind?"

"Of course."

"Well, you know, I still think it would be good for me to go somewhere, and the Chicago fair is all done."

"Yes, and I'm sorry. It's my fault you didn't get to go."

"Let's not worry about that. It's gone. But I still have the idea that I should take a trip somewhere, for myself."

"Where are you thinking of going?"

"To France."

"Really?"

"Well, you know I've always wanted to go there."

"Yes, I know that, but—"

"But?"

"I always thought, after we'd talked about it so many times, that we'd go there on our honeymoon."

"My God," he said. "Do you still think that's possible?"

"What have we talked about?"

"Actually, we've talked about a great many things. But I haven't gotten a sense that anything is going to happen very soon."

"Something's going to have to, sooner or later."

"Well, I can't do it. That is, I can't push it. It would be wrong with everyone."

"I know. We've already talked about that."

He sensed an impatience. "I know you need to go. But I needed just a minute or two here. Isn't it possible to tell him and get things out in the open?"

She pulled him to her and kissed him. "I need to wait a little longer."

"Sometimes I think we've waited way past the moment, and the best thing would be for me to bow out."

"Do you want to?"

"No, I don't, but I don't know if you want me to."

"I don't want you to. I need you." She kissed him again, then tapped him on the nose and said, "I'm sorry, but I have to go before someone gets an idea."

He was back in his room at seven-thirty. By his estimation, taking into account the time he had gotten there, the amount of time he stood waiting, and the amount it took to walk back, they had spent a maximum of seven minutes together.

CHAPTER SIX

From the outside, the house looked close to completion. Collier had gotten the roof nailed on and the sideboards put up. According to Tom Sedley, Quist in his spare time had helped put the windows in place and hang the doors. Lane doubted that Collier would be able to paint the exterior before the cold weather set in for good, but there was plenty of work to do on the inside. Through the front window Lane could see bare studs on the interior walls. For as much as he didn't care for Collier and his dark scowls, he didn't begrudge him the comfort of working inside and avoiding the worst of the weather.

Lane went on his way, walking at random as had become his custom. He liked to be seen out at different hours, walking different patterns. He had come to enjoy his walks in and for themselves, and at this time of the year when the days were at their shortest, Sunday afternoon was the time when he could get out and see how the world was inching along.

As he meandered through the town, his route took him within a block of Emma's house, where Joseph Saxton, in his high-crowned, narrow-brimmed hat, was handing the schoolteacher up the front steps. There was another man he couldn't begrudge, in spite of his selfish retreat. If, as Tom Sedley had mentioned, Joseph was negotiating a price on the house Collier was building, Lane wished him well. Take plump little Frances and plump her up some more. Make the world go around.

Lane stood outside the back door of the office, waiting for Cora. He would rather have been standing inside, where some of the workday's warmth would still be lingering, but the back of the office had no windows looking out. So he stood in the cold, trying to be still.

She said sometime between seven and eight. He had been on the spot since a few minutes before seven, and now his feet were cold. He unlocked the door and stepped inside to the warmth. He lit a match and looked at his watch. Seven-fifteen. Sometime between seven and eight. That meant he would wait until eight-thirty. And after that? He could wait five minutes more, or pack his bags for France, or take some other method of self-defense. Knock on Madeline Edgeworth's door.

He looked out into the night. Nothing. His feet were still cold, so he walked up and down the hallway a dozen times. He looked out the door, took another dozen turns in the hallway. Looked out again.

Seven-thirty. He had to consider the possibility that she might not come at all, that something went wrong. A few more turns in the hallway. *Don't count them.*

He stood in one place and moved his arms back and forth. He took off his gloves and held his hands to his face. Warm. He cracked the door open again and looked out, felt the cold air on his face. He went back to walking. It was only warm inside by comparison.

Seven-forty. He imagined too many scenarios, like before. McGavin with a shotgun, Cora at his feet. Rox Barlow, nervous at the sight of a gun muzzle, opening the door of Lane's room and turning to shake his head. He's not here. Cora serving a glass of whiskey and then sitting by the tub and listening to the master tell how he was going to make his million.

The aggrieved husband sitting his family down by the fire and saying, Children, I have something to tell you about your mother.

And again, the large man coming through the front door with a six-gun leveled.

Five minutes to eight. A boiling in his guts, a dull fire reaching farther down. *Put the gloves back on, walk some more.*

Ten past eight. Somewhere in this town, something had gone wrong. She was going to use Emma for an alibi, but she hadn't cleared it with

Emma. Maybe McGee went there. Maybe he didn't let her go anywhere. Sit down, children.

Cora stretched out on the floor, an arm flung to the side. Rat poison she should have put in the man's hotcakes.

Sit down, you're not going anywhere. Pour me a drink.

He opened the door and felt the cold night again. He lit a match. Eight-seventeen. He picked up all the dead matches and took them to the stove, tossed them in on the faint embers.

Emma and her husband standing inside the door. No, she didn't say anything to me. Cora ladling soup to Franklin and Belinda. Your father said it's not a good night for anyone to go out, so we'll all just use the thunder mug. And he cut off the head of the witch and took her tinderbox.

The fire he had never felt before, deep down, that wouldn't go away. Walk and walk and walk, and it didn't go away.

He stalled as long as he could until he looked at his watch again. It was eight thirty-five. He was as washed out as if he had been begging with the executioner, a tall hooded man with a double-edged sword.

Out into the night again, he walked to her end of town. The house was dark except for one light in back. It was not yet nine o'clock, and under reasonable circumstances it was not too late to ask someone. But Emma was in hot water already, and unless McGee went there, which would make another visit disastrous, she would know nothing.

Then on a hunch he went to Mrs. Canby's house and knocked on the door.

"No, honey," she said, her voice full of sympathy. "I haven't heard nothin'."

Then it was back to his room for a sleepless, thirsty night, a fire that wouldn't go away, and a fear in his guts that something had gone wrong.

In the morning, St. John was waiting for him at the office. Lane thought the stern demeanor had something to do with his having been there the night before, but St. John surprised him with a different tack.

"Lane, I'm letting you go. I think you probably know why, but I'd rather have no misunderstandings." St. John shifted his backside at the stove. "You've been a good man at your work, and I've got no complaints about it. But the nature of my dealings with other men, as you know, requires a sterling impression. I wouldn't want anyone to be able to question the integrity of this office in any way. Again, you've been a good man in my employ, but I've got my public reasons for doing what I have to do."

It sounded well rehearsed, everything already decided and worked out. "I see. Is there anything you'd like me to finish up?"

"I'd just as soon you didn't."

"Then I guess you'd like this." Lane handed him the key, and without having taken off his hat and coat, he walked back out into the cold morning.

* * *

He felt as if he were falling into a deep chasm. Then without hitting bottom he was on his feet, groping, still in the dark. Something had happened, something beyond his understanding. He was a blind man swinging a cane.

He took refuge first in his room and then in language. Pen and paper. It was the one thing he could do, the one way he found the power to act.

He wrote a long letter, six pages, stating his full case—how he should have done more, how he restrained himself from forcing a decision, how he would not desert her if she needed him, and how he would bow out if it made things easier. He played with the phrase "some honor left," then changed it to "I have yet some measure of honor." He wrote of the lone winter he found himself, then stated that he brought it upon himself and would take his drubbing without complaint. Closing on a positive note, he borrowed the phrase "hope springs eternal" and said he hoped to see her again "when the long winter breaks."

Reviewing it, he thought he did justice to all the points he had rehearsed of late, and he felt he had phrased all of his ideas rather well. After he had read the letter through a second time, he decided it had done all the good it was going to do. He was struck with the futility of trying to change anything this way, or even of trying to place the letter in her hands, so he burned it in the cast-iron stove in the hotel lobby.

* * *

After a full week of silence, during which time he alternated between self-pity and bitterness, he received a note through Mrs. Canby. Cora said she could meet him at the dressmaker's in the middle of the day. Not knowing what to expect and not having any other claim on his time, Lane went there. He knocked on the back door and was let into the room, where in a short while he saw Cora.

She was wearing the white blouse with buttons the color of an apothecary bottle, and her eyes were deeper blue than the willowware. Her dark hair hung at her shoulders as before, but she had a somber, bereaved air about her. If she had been shorn like a lamb she could not have looked more defeated.

When he reached to take her hands, she pulled them back. Then he saw that she was trying to hide them. They were rough, scaly with rash. He sat her down on the bed next to him, took one hand, and rubbed it.

"What's the matter?"

"All nerves. Tension. I haven't been able to go anywhere or be by myself for a moment."

"I wrote you a letter, but it seemed so pointless. And I didn't know how to get it to you. Or if you could even have it."

She looked down and shook her head.

"What happened?"

She sobbed. "He found out."

"I assumed that. But I was wondering how it all happened."

"Oh, Lane, it was terrible. He found your letters, all your beautiful letters, and the flowers you drew and the little verses you wrote. And he burned them. All of them. And the book of poems. Everything."

Gone. He suppressed saying that he had warned her. And for all he knew, she might have allowed the letters to bring out the truth without her having to make a move. "How did he find them?"

"Franklin told him. He saw me putting one away."

"And so everything blew up?"

"Not right away. He found the letters and took them. I didn't know yet. I didn't check on them every day. And then he let me go to Emma's. I should have been suspicious when he didn't ask me anything. But he let me go, just like walking into a trap. Before I got very far, he came in the buggy and told me to get in. He asked me what I had to do at Emma's. I said talk. He said I didn't need to be talking woman talk when I had things to take care of at home. I knew what he meant. I hadn't let him come near me for some time."

"I didn't know that."

"No, you never asked, you dear boy."

"So you went back home in the buggy?"

"No. He took me somewhere else. Away from the children. He took me to the house he's having built, and he took me inside and—did it to me, on the bare floor. He said if I could give it to someone else, I could give it to him."

"You mean he—?"

"Yes, he took me. Against my will. After that, everything went dark. It was as if I was seeing through a pair of pinholes, and my children's voices were far away."

"He took you home, then."

"Yes. I barely remember getting into the house. He told the children I was sick. Then the next day, when I was coming out of it, he told the children to go in the other room. That was when he burned everything and boasted. He had read all the letters, he knew everything. He told me I could stay away from the window from now on, because he knew what it meant. And he told me not to be leaving any more notes under my favorite rock, but he wasn't moving it because he wanted to see if he could catch any fish."

"Is that what he's been doing for the past week, then—watching the fishing hole?"

"Not exactly. But he hasn't gone out much."

"Doesn't he have to work?"

"He's selling that house to Joseph, so he got some earnest money to keep him for a while."

"So does he just sit in your lap?"

"Almost. He's gone out to talk to other people, but he leaves Franklin."

"Other people."

"He went to see Douglas Apley and got him to say a few words to me about rash actions."

"That's sweet. He drags you through the mud with your friends as well as your children."

"Douglas told me he wouldn't want me to think he took it upon himself."

"So McGee was making the rounds. I gather he spoke with my employer, or I should say, my ex-employer."

"Yes, he was pleased with that. And later on, Mr. St. John came to talk to me and told me how he hoped I didn't err any further or do any greater damage to my family."

"What do you think about that?"

"He's a very proper man."

"I meant, about what he said. About your doing anything further."

"I don't know."

"I suppose it's hard to disagree with someone who's such a paragon. I'm sure he's easier to take than this other sanctimonious fellow with all his posturing. By the way, does he know you came here today?"

"No. Franklin will probably tell him I was gone, but I don't care. I had to see you one more time."

Things sounded rather final. He rubbed her hand. "Did you . . . impose any conditions on yourself before you came here?"

"No," she said, turning her eyes to him. They were lighter blue now, and swimming in tears. "I want to be yours, one more time."

Afterward, when they were calm and lying side by side, she said, "He thinks it's all over, just because he found out and smeared it everywhere. And did what he did."

"What a fool. He can't touch us, not with what

we have. We put everything back together again. Don't you think?"

"It sure felt like it."

"Do you think you have to go back, at least for a little while?"

She gave him a cold stare. "I don't know what else I can do."

"You mean, things are not over between us, but you'll have to go back to him and be treated worse than ever?"

"What else can I do?"

"I don't know. A thousand things. For one, you could come to me."

Her eyes filled with tears again. "I'm sorry. I can't. Not after all of this."

"It might be the best time, when things are kicked wide open."

"Oh, Lane. If you knew what he told me when he burned everything!"

"Maybe I should hear it."

"He said that if I ever tried to leave him, he would see to it that I never saw my children again."

"Do you think he could do that?"

"I don't know."

"But you don't want to find out."

"I just wish there were two of me."

He wanted to say, "It seems as if you tried that, and it didn't work at all." But he wasn't sure he understood in what way she meant it. "You haven't really decided, have you?" he asked.

"No."

"But you're going back all the same."

"I really don't have any choice."

"That leaves me out in the cold, but I can take care of myself. You knew you could count on me to take my medicine, didn't you?"

"Yes, you lovely boy. I knew I could."

Lane sat in his room, staring at the walls, the curtains, the door. With the bitter weather and short days, plus a general listlessness, he had gone out hardly at all since the day St. John had fired him. He had a bit of money saved up, so he didn't have to worry about how he was going to pay his keep through the winter. And as long as Cora was in town, he wasn't going to take any trips. He had time, far more than he needed, to sort things out.

No one dies of love. No one dies of a broken heart. He had heard that wisdom many times, and he imagined now that he had gotten it from people who had not taken the fall he had. People who had not been knocked out of balance inside, with the spleen and the liver and who knew what, all out of their proper order. Low energy, low ambition, melancholy. Something in the blood.

He didn't care to read, and after the one outpouring that he burned, he didn't care to write. He thought of passages he had read, parts of poems and plays, and he thought of mournful songs in which people did die of love. One of them, "Bonny Barbara Allan," came to him in full, and he sang it in low tones. He was quite sure he was doing what thousands of others had done, in taverns and on their own—merging with the maudlin emotion and finding something real in the story in spite of the excess. If there were a saloon nearby, as there were in the East, where Irish laborers met to hoist a pint of bitters, he would join them and be like all the others.

He did not think he would see Cora again—not very soon, at least—but about a week after their meeting at Mrs. Canby's, a note came to him at the hotel desk. Emma had taken great pity on her and had agreed to let her meet with him in her living room, at a time when Douglas and the schoolteacher would both be away. Ten in the morning, if he wanted to see her.

Hoping not to be the first to arrive, he made a point of being ten minutes late. Cora was standing in front of the sofa when Emma opened the door, and at first glance he could see she was further gone than the last time he had seen her.

"How have you been?" he asked, as soon as Emma had gone into the kitchen.

"All right, I guess. And yourself? Oh, why do I ask, when I know I've ruined you?"

"Don't worry about me. Look out for yourself."

Her eyes went down. "I'm the last person who deserves it."

"Wait a minute," he said. "How many more people have been pummeling you?"

"Oh, not that many."

He gave her a sharp look. "Has someone done something more to you?"

"Actually, he's been rather nice to me, to give him his due."

"Has he apologized, or in any way made amends?"

"No. He took me to Cheyenne, and we stayed in a hotel. He went out and bought me dresses and jewelry, things I would never have chosen for myself."

Lane felt a queasy wave spreading through his abdomen. "So he just went out and bought all these things, and you accepted them?"

"I wasn't in any position to reject them."

Lane said nothing.

"I'm sorry," she said, breaking into sobs.

"For that? For accepting his . . . gifts?"

She raised her eyes, and her face was full of agony. "I had to give myself back to him."

"You mean—"

"He went out and found a minister, and he wanted to make me renew my wedding vows. I balked on that, but finally I gave in as far as the other part goes." She sobbed and sounded as if she was going to choke. "I'm sorry."

"I'll tell you again. Look out for yourself. If you have to go back to your husband, that's what you have to do. But protect your own dignity in whatever way you can. Try to keep some position for yourself. At this point, I can't care. I simply can't. If he wants to buy you back with money he can ill afford—I suppose he's dribbled away all the earnest money on the house, and I know for a fact that he still owes for all the lumber. Or did before all of this happened."

After a long moment, she said, "Actually, he got the money from me."

"What's that?"

"I had my own little cache of money. I had scrimped and saved here and there, and every once in a while I would put back a little bit. In case I ever needed it, to take the children somewhere out of danger, I don't know. But I had it. Almost two hundred dollars."

"Did he know about it?"

"He found it when he went through all my things."

Lane shook his head and let out a long breath. "What did he say?"

"Nothing."

"He just took it, and you found out it was gone."

"Yes."

"Did you say anything to him about it?"

She shook her head.

"And did you ever hold him accountable for anything else he did? For example, when he took you to that house? Have you ever brought it up?"

She shook her head.

"It would have been a good thing to tell that minister." He looked at her. "But I don't suppose you could. This fellow's got you keeping his secrets for him."

"You tell me," she said. "I don't know anything anymore."

"My God, Cora, no matter what you've done, you can't let this fellow walk all over you. There'll be no end to it. What kind of a life do you think you're going back into?"

Her throat sounded swollen. "What I deserve."

"He'll hold all of this over you forever."

"Time heals all wounds. That's what he says."

"Was that some kind of an assurance?"

"No, not really. He said it when I told him I didn't know how I could give you up."

"Well, he might tell you that, but don't count on him taking it to heart himself."

"Do you think I can give you up?"

"It sounds as if you have."

"Why do you think I had to see you again? Oh, Lane, I will never forget you, never quit loving you until I draw my last breath. He can never take away the memories I have, or what you've meant to me."

"And yet you go back into bondage. You said the other day you had no choice."

"I don't see where I do."

"Then I don't suppose we'll meet again in the near future."

"I don't think so. He says he's taking us all away."

Small, dry snowflakes were falling as he walked back to his room. It was over, and it was not over. She had no choice, but by doing nothing she had made a choice. McGee could take her money, take her body against her will, degrade her with other people and bring them in to batter down her resistance, and he was justified. Cora didn't have a word. Nor did he, Lane Weller, the man who had raised his hand against another man's marriage. That was how it was all defined.

All the same, he had nothing to complain about.

As he had written in the ephemeral letter, he brought it on himself. Whatever was going to be done, he was going to have to do it himself. He did not feel as if he were falling anymore, or that he was a blind man swinging a cane, but he was in a dark place, feeling his way against a wall of stone.

Tom Sedley set a mug of beer on the bar. "Come out of hibernation, huh?"

"Might as well."

"Life goes on, for the lucky."

"I'll agree with that much, even if I feel like Moses when the lights went out. And there are worse shoes to be in than mine."

Sedley gave him a nod with a knowing look.

"She says he's taking them all away."

"That's the word. Packin' up and goin' somewhere else. But he's not sellin' the house."

"The one they live in."

"Right."

"Any reason why?"

"Supposedly so they can come back whenever he feels like it. Could be just a way of savin' face, to say that no one made him leave."

"Maybe so. Or to keep others guessing. I understand he tends to leave things hanging."

The door of the saloon opened, and Newt Collier took a place at the end of the bar. Sedley made a flick with his eyebrows and went to serve him.

Lane glanced in the mirror and saw Collier, drawing himself up to his full height but still not tall. The man looked stocky in his winter coat and round-brimmed hat, and he seemed to flex his muscles as he laid a coin on the bar.

Sedley poured the drink and took the coin. As he was putting it in the cash box, Collier's voice called out.

"Tom, do you know anyone who's looking for work?"

The bartender looked over his shoulder. "No, I don't."

"Huh. I heard there were a few men out of work."

"I don't know."

"Well, if you hear of anyone, let me know."

Lane drank down his beer and pushed his mug away. "I don't think this is doing me as much good as it should. I'll come back when the weather's better."

Tom nodded.

Lane had to pass within a few feet of Collier as he walked to the door. When he was just past the man, the voice came.

"I heard you were lookin' for work, Mr. Weller."

Lane paused. "I don't know who would have told you that."

They were facing each other now. Lane could see the dark mustache and stubble.

"It's a good job. Fittin' shoes for women. Kneelin' at their feet. Your kind of work."

Lane started to move, but the voice held him.

"Or carryin' bags in a hotel. For those guests that have bags. Who knows who you might meet?"

"Go to hell."

Collier's hand came up out of nowhere and slapped him on the cheek.

Sedley called out from down the bar, "Hey, none of that in here."

"That's fine," said Collier. "We're takin' it outside." He motioned with his hat toward the door. "Go ahead."

Lane stepped into the cold night, where light flakes were still falling. He couldn't see a way out of this one. The last thing he was going to do was let someone call him a coward. Even if it meant—

Collier's fist caught him before he had even decided how to square off. His feet went out from under him on the slick sidewalk, and he landed with his rump on the boards.

"Get up."

He shifted up onto his elbows, in no hurry for the next part.

"Get up, you pot-licker." Collier leaned over, grabbed him by the front of his coat, and jerked him to his feet. The next punch put him in the street.

Lane's cheek and jaw throbbed with a sharp ache, and the world was tilted. Collier hauled him up again. This time he punched him in the stomach.

Snow falling in his face, his hat gone somewhere. Collier's voice taunting.

"You're damn lucky someone didn't do you a lot worse. Damn lucky. Men get killed for what you did."

The street felt frozen to the touch. He put the

heel of his hand on a rock and pushed himself up into a sitting position. Light through the window of the saloon showed him where his hat lay flat on the white sidewalk.

Tom Sedley came out wearing a heavy wool coat. He reached down and helped Lane to his feet.

"Do you need anything?"

"Not right now, Tom. I think I'm all right. Just let me clear my head for a minute."

Tom brought him his hat.

"Thanks. I think I'm better off alone for a few minutes."

"All right." Tom went back into the saloon.

Lane stood in the street, gazing into the winter night beyond the edge of town. Did he need anything? He guessed he did.

CHAPTER SEVEN

The singsong voices of the other workers floated on the air. Chatter, chatter, all the words running together, now and then a laugh. Lane jabbed with his shovel, carving downward, then switched it around to scoop, lift, and toss. Good weather to learn this kind of work. Not too hot, not too cold. Too early for snakes. Good work, too. Put muscle on a man. Gave him time to think, play over scenes and words and phrases. Little verses.

When Adam delved and Eve span,
Who was then a gentleman?

The others left him to himself. A few words of English, a few words of Spanish—it didn't take much to get across a handful of simple ideas. Clean the deetchee, payday too-night, no work tomorrow. Son of a beetchee, doña Veekee, ha-ha-ha.

A merry crew. Lane squatted with them around the sagebrush fire as the one called Memo heated tortillas on a cast-iron griddle and handed them out. Tabo spooned beans and bacon ends from a Dutch oven onto tin plates. When his meal was served, Lane took a seat with his back against a wagon wheel.

There was an old song he couldn't dredge up. Something about fifteen miles on the Erie Canal. That would have been when they had water in it. The crew was making a little bit better than a mile a day on this one. It would be another month or more until they turned the water into it, up at the weir or whatever they called it out here.

The old man Miguel, who drove the wagon, was sitting against the other half of the wheel. "You pretty good to shoot?" he asked, holding out his arms in the position of firing a rifle.

"No, not very good."

Miguel went on to tell, in broken English, how a young man came by last year and gave them some antelope meat. He came three or four times. Good cowboy. Neek.

A couple of days later, when they had pitched the tents for the evening but were still loafing around the campfire, five of the six Mexicans smoking cigarettes, a rider came to their camp. Amidst the muttering, Lane picked out the sound "Neek. Neek."

The rider stopped a few yards out and swung down. He looked like a happy-go-lucky young fellow, somewhere in his early twenties. He was fitted out like all the cowhands Lane was used to seeing, with vest, neckerchief, six-gun, boots, and spurs.

"Hey, Miguel," he said. "I brought you some meat." He pointed at a canvas bundle tied on the back of his saddle. "Carny."

"Oh, thass gude," said Miguel, who had gotten to his feet and had come to shake the young man's hand. Then he spoke in Spanish to a couple of the men lounging on their bedrolls, and they got up.

The young rider nodded for the two men to untie the bundle. With his reins in one hand and his other thumb on his belt, he glanced around the camp until his eyes lit on Lane. "Well, hello there. Didn't see you at first. You workin' with this bunch?"

Lane got up to talk to the cowboy. "Yes, I am."

"Good bunch. You been at it long?"

"A little over a week."

"How do you like it?"

"It's work." He ran his thumb across the underside of his hand, where the blisters were turning to calluses. "Sort of new to me, this kind of work, but I'm gettin' used to it."

The young man gave a quick look at his clothes and nodded. "My name's Nick Robison," he said, holding out his hand. He was of average height, eyes level with his new acquaintance.

"I'm Lane Weller."

"Pleased to meet you, Lane."

"You work on a ranch here?"

"I sure do. Fella by the name of Nance Fredman. Has the Rosette Ranch. Over on the other side of that butte." He gave Lane an appraising look. "You ever do ranch work?"

"Not much."

"Well, if you can learn to work with a nigger hoe and a shovel with these fellows, you can learn ranch work. Can you keep from fallin' off a horse?"

"Most of the time."

"Well, I'll tell you what. The old man'll probably be puttin' on a couple more hands in another week or so. If you have some way of gettin' out there, you could see about it."

"I might try that."

Nick held out his hand. "Well, it's good to meet you, Lane."

"Same here. Just on the other side of that butte?"

"That's right. You can't miss it."

Nance Fredman was a leathered and wrinkled old man, short and thin with a hatchet face, an eagle nose, and a few gaps where teeth used to be. He had old-age spots on the backs of his hands, and his right index finger was missing.

"Nick tells me you want to be a hand."

"I'd like to try it."

"What don't you like about the work you're doin?"

"It's not going to last much longer, and I'd like a job through the season."

"Where did you work before you got on with the ditch crew?"

He knew he would have to answer that question. "I used to work for Wilson St. John, in his office."

"What did you not like about that job?"

"Nothing. He let me go. One of his friends didn't like me."

"Heh! One of his friends don't like me, either. But I don't give a good goddamn." He squinted. "I'll tell ya, I ain't got no ass-sittin' jobs."

"I'm not looking for one."

"This other job toughen you up a little?"

Lane's muscles tensed beneath his shirt. "A little."

Nance looked him up and down. "Well, you might make a hand. You still look a little like one of them bone-huntin' bugologists, but I think Nick can take that out of you. How'd you get here?"

"I rode one of the horses from the ditch crew. Another man rode over with me."

"You got a bedroll?"

"Yes, sir."

"Then you can roll it out in the bunkhouse, and tell your friend he can go back. Are you all squared up with them fellers?"

"Yes, sir. I just got paid up."

"Were you in the army?"

"No, sir."

"Neither was I. Good way to get the clap, goin' to places where they've been."

"I believe it."

"So I was wonderin' why you called me 'sir.' "

"I have no idea."

"We eat off the same stick and drink out of the same canteen here."

"Just the way I like it."

"Good. Now you go see Nick."

* * *

The loop sailed over the horse's head as he turned away. Lane thought it would miss, but it caught. Nick pulled his slack and braced both of his heels in the dirt. As the other two horses ran to the far corner of the corral, Nick squared around in front of the sorrel and braced himself again.

"Here," he said, when the horse quit pulling back. He handed the rope to Lane, then walked to the corral gate.

Lane held the coils in one hand and snugged up with the other as he led the horse out of the corral.

"Let's put a halter on him," Nick said when they got to the hitching rail, where a rope halter with lead rope was dangling on the far end. He slipped the halter onto the horse's head, took off the long rope, and tied the lead rope to the rail. Then he untied it and showed Lane how to tie the release knot. "You'll need to learn how to rope out your own horses," he said, "but you can't learn it all in a day. We'll start with this part. You know how to brush and saddle him?"

"I know that much."

"All right. You'll need spurs, but everything in its good time." He took a brush out of his hip pocket and handed it to Lane. "Eventually the old man'll expect you to ride any horse on the ranch. He still does it himself. Tough as an old boot. But he doesn't keep any outlaws around. Puts a bullet through their head, or has me do it."

"Horses."

"Yeh. That's what they call 'em. Outlaws. You'll see a draw where we take 'em."

* * *

Nick started him out roping on the ground with a dummy made out of a stump.

"You practice this for about half an hour every day," he said. "When you get to catchin' most of the time, move back a little. Get this part down. Then everything changes when you get on a horse, and your calf or your steer is moving."

Next he showed him how to tie a calf. "Flank it down first, get the piggin' string on the bottom hoof, lay the other two on top, give 'er three wraps and a hooey, and there you are."

He showed him again when they needed to get a cow and a calf back to the home corral. They tied the calf and put it in the bed of the wagon. The mother followed, mooing and drooling. Whenever the trussed calf started flopping around too much, Lane pulled up on the piggin' string. Three wraps and a hooey. Nice little system of bondage.

One morning when he had been at the ranch about a week, Lane saw Nick take a rifle and scabbard from the wall.

"The old man wants me to get some meat for the Mexicans. He says you can go along."

As they rode out of the ranch a half hour later, Lane said, "He must like these fellows, to look after 'em this way."

"Not so much. They're just like any other workin' men to him. But if he takes 'em meat, they understand not to kill any of his beef."

"What are we after today?"

"Whatever we find. Antelope are easier to find, and deer are easier to kill. You can get up closer on 'em."

About an hour away from the ranch, Nick drew rein at the edge of the draw. "See that deer down there in the brush?"

Lane squinted and strained, then made out a patch of dull color amidst a tangle of dry branches. "Oh, yeh."

"Well, we're not gonna shoot at it." He looked across at Lane. "For one, you can't see the whole thing. It might be a doe with a fawn. For another, I don't like to shoot a deer in its bed. I just don't care for it. I did it one time, early on, and when I walked up to it I found out it had already been dead for a day or two. I didn't feel like much of a hunter. And it just seems fairer to let 'em stand up first." He sat with both hands on the saddle horn for a long minute and said, "Let's go ahead, and see if it moves."

He nudged his horse down the draw, and Lane followed. When they reached the bottom, the deer got up from its bed and tramped out through the dry twigs.

"Aw, it's just a yearling doe," said Nick. "We'll find something else."

Half an hour later, Nick led them up a grassy slope behind a rock outcropping. He dismounted and signaled for Lane to do the same. When the two of them were standing close together, he spoke in a low voice.

"This is a good place for antelope. You hold the

horses and watch me. See how I go up slow, so as not to run out of breath. If I see something, I want a steady shot, not wobblin' around."

He pulled the rifle from his scabbard and started toward the brow of the hill. He took slow steps, inching his head upward, and then he sank back. After levering in a shell, he moved a few paces to his right and crept up behind the rock. He brought the rifle around and settled into position. Lane was impressed with how still he held.

The rifle crashed, and Nick jerked with the recoil. Then he lowered the gun and turned around, smiling. "Meat on the ground."

As they rode down the slope on the other side, Lane picked out the tan body and white underside of the fallen animal. Closer, he saw that it had horns about five inches high. Blood glistened out of a hole behind the front leg and above the sternum.

"Do you know how to dress 'em?" Nick asked.

"No, I don't."

"Well, I guess we'll learn that, too."

Elbert Maude showed up a couple of days later. He was a loose-jointed kid, about eighteen or nineteen. When he introduced himself to Lane, he said he was from Tennessee and had worked on the ranch "laist year." For the rest of the evening, he made comments implying that he had seniority over Lane.

Nance still treated him as a kid. "Fer God's sake, Elbert, tuck in yer shirt. Go around lookin' like a bumpkin." When they were working on a branding corral and Elbert left the crowbar in the dirt, Nance sent him back for it, but not without a chewing-out. "Damn you, Elbert, you need to learn to quit droppin' things at your ass." But he did anyway. He left a feed bucket out in the yard, a saddle blanket on the corral rail. Once when the four of them were resting at midday, ten miles out where a trickle of water ran through a patch of box elders, they tied their horses with neck ropes and wrapped the reins around the saddle horns. Of the four horses, Elbert's had one rein drooping lower than the other, by six inches. Nance let out a huff of disgust, got up onto his feet, and walked over to the horse. "Fer God's sake, Elbert. Even if *no* one else is around to see it, tie your reins even." Nance adjusted the reins and rewound them. Elbert, with his hat back on his head, looked up with his heavy-lidded gaze.

A few days after that, Nance sent Elbert and Lane out together. Lane had his doubts to begin with, but he understood that the old man, like other cattlemen, liked to send his riders out two together, and he wanted Nick to ride with him that day.

Elbert did most of the talking for the first two miles out, mentioning from time to time how they had done things "laist year." When it came time to split up, he said they could meet at Squaw Rock in about two hours. Lane said he knew where it was, about two miles west and three miles north, to the west of some white clay bluffs.

"That's it," said Elbert. "You cain't miss it."

Lane was careful riding out. As for not being

able to miss a landmark, he would never have found the Rosette Ranch if Memo had not gone along with him. Since he had been at the ranch, he had had a few small incidents in which Nick or Nance had told him how to find a place, and he had reviewed the directions before starting out. He would still have to backtrack and ride in big circles to find something as simple as a water hole. This time he was pretty sure he knew where Squaw Rock was, but he watched the country both ahead and behind, he kept an eye on the sun overhead, and he looked at his watch every ten or fifteen minutes. At the same time, he was looking for cattle so he could give Nance a count.

He found Squaw Rock all right, with time to spare. In his eyes it didn't look much like a squaw, just a crooked column of sandstone, but Nick said it was so named because someone, at some time, thought it looked like a squaw carrying a papoose. Its best feature at the present was its wide base, which cast a large enough shadow for Lane and his horse.

Time passed, and the shadows inched out onto the grassland. Lane began to feel the familiar uneasiness of waiting for someone. This was different, though. Elbert was just sloppy. He'd be moseying over the hill in a little while.

Lane looked at his watch. It was four o'clock, a full hour past the meeting time. If he wanted to get back to the ranch at a reasonable hour, he might as well start now. He could poke around in the vicinity to see if he could find Elbert, and he would line out at five.

One thing he had learned about the range country. Any part of it was much bigger than it looked like from even a short distance. Within a few minutes he was off into a part of it he had never seen before, a large grassy bowl with side canyons fingering off between tall, narrow bluffs. He looked at the sun, got his bearings, and decided to go back the way he came. He rode up the slope and then cut northeast to follow a passageway that angled through a high clay wall.

Before he came out on the other side, he met Newt Collier.

It was the man with the dark mustache and dark eyes, all right, but he was way out of place. And following from about a half mile back. Nothing made sense except that someone who didn't like Lane had shown up to give him trouble.

It looked as if they might be able to ride past one another without rubbing legs, but there was no way around a confrontation. At a distance of ten yards, Collier spoke.

"Well, look who we've got here. Are you lost?"

"I could ask the same of you."

"Don't worry about me, sonny boy. But you look like you're off your range."

"Not here, I'm not. If it's anything to you, I'm working for the Rosette."

"Well, good for you. Found a job, did you?"

"Yes, and I don't have to carry someone else's water for him."

"Spoken with pride." Collier, who was wearing gauntlet-type gloves with long cuffs, took off one and then the other and held them in his left hand. He transferred the reins to his right hand.

"And yourself?"

"Like I said, don't worry about me. But when our outfits come together at roundup, you can satisfy your curiosity."

"That's a prospect to look forward to." Lane tried to gauge the passageway. "But if there's not much more to talk about now, I've got work to do."

"Sure. Go right on by. Plenty of room."

Lane nudged his horse forward. The animal balked and tried to turn, so he hit it with his heels again. The horse straightened out, then tried to turn. Lane used his heels and wished he had spurs.

The horse straightened out again and took slow steps forward. Lane could feel himself on edge, and he hoped he didn't transfer any fear to the horse.

Forward some more. Very slow. The two horses tipped their heads away from one another. Lane's horse moved deeper into the gap. As the two riders came opposite one another, Lane did not look at his antagonist. Rather, he kept his eye on the haunch of the other horse.

"Why, you ride just like a regular cowpuncher."

Lane said nothing. He kept his gaze fixed ahead.

Out of nowhere, the heavy gloves came with a stinging slap on the back of his head, and his hat fell off as his horse bolted. It crow-hopped half a dozen times. Lane grabbed for the saddle horn and lost it, then lost his left stirrup, bounced in and out of the seat, lost his right stirrup, and landed in the dirt on the left side of his sashaying horse. Through it all he held on to one rein, and when he hit the ground he still had it. Up on his feet, he got in front of the horse as he had seen Nick do. He grabbed two or three times for the other rein until he caught it. Then the horse settled down.

Lane looked up at the cleft in the wall. His hat was lying on the trail, and Collier was gone. In no hurry to climb back on, Lane led the horse up the hill, retrieved his hat, and got the reins into position. Then he thought better of it, led the horse down to a flat spot, and mounted up. Once in the saddle, he pulled his hat down tight and gave the horse some rein. He let out a long breath. At least he didn't have to walk back to the ranch.

At supper, Elbert seemed nonchalant about not having met at the appointed place. He said he went close by, didn't see Lane, and went on about his ride. "Ah figgered, if you didn't see me, you'd know enough to come back on your own." Lane wouldn't have minded having a long pair of gloves himself at that moment, but he said no more. And in spite of Elbert's authority, he suspected that the kid might not have been able to find Squaw Rock.

A little later, when Lane had a moment with Nick, he asked him if he knew which outfit Collier worked for.

"I think I know the fella you mean, but I don't know who he might be ridin' with. Did you see the brand on the horse?"

"I didn't think to notice."

"Well, roundup'll be startin' real soon, and we'll find out then."

To give Nick some idea of what to expect when they did meet Collier at a chuck wagon, Lane told him that Collier seemed to be carrying someone else's grudge. He gave a summary of the fight in town and a brief account of the meeting out on the trail.

"Sounds like a fella who thinks he's smart. It would do him some good to have his wolf teeth pulled."

"What's that?"

"Oh, when you geld a horse, you pull a pair of teeth on top so the bit'll sit in there proper."

"Sounds like just the thing for the fellow he used to work for, too. The trouble is, their kind don't get their comeuppance often enough. They get things their way, cheat to do it, and get away with it."

Nick smiled. "Like Nance says, the world is full of sons of bitches, and you just try to see how many you can outlive. Me, I try to stay away from 'em."

Lane smiled back. "So do I, but they have a way of finding me."

Lane gazed at the stars as he felt the horse poke along beneath him. It was slow and calm tonight, like most nights had been. Here and there the tinkle of a horse bell, no two of them alike. A snuffle-snort, a stamp on the earth. Ride the slow circle around.

Night wrangler. Lowest rank of all the jobs on roundup. No complaints, though. Good for a beginner. Gave a man time alone, time to think.

During the day, when he was helping the cook move the wagons and gather firewood, men were coming in to change mounts, grab a bite, or get something out of the bed wagon. Hubbub all the time. Sometimes he got hardly any sleep under the wagon, and then it was a drowsy night. Not tonight, though. He felt awake and clearheaded.

Not a day went by that he didn't think of Cora, who knows how many times? But when he was alone at night, looking at the sky, he thought of her most and of the best times they'd had together. Add it all up, the slivers of time over less than a year, and it wasn't a great deal. Even that whole year, stacked against all the years that went before and those that would come after, didn't count as very much. But it was bigger than anything that ever happened to him, and it hadn't died. Somewhere out there, under a roof under this same sky, she would be sleeping. She probably wasn't happy a good part of the time, and even though she had the company of her husband and children, she probably felt as he did, that a person had to get through problems alone.

He could remember the first time he had expressed that idea out loud. It was early on, in Emma's living room, before he and Cora ever kissed. The two of them were talking about the ways of the country. She said life was desolate, and he said a person had to work on things alone. They had understood each other from the beginning; their thoughts fit together like two halves of an orange. And the part about being alone had proven true.

The West was a good place for people to pitch in and help when trouble struck. He had seen that. If a man broke a leg, lost his barn in a fire, or got hailed out, the neighbors came along and helped him get through it. They cared for his stock, rebuilt the barn, lent good cheer. But if the problem was the kind that he and Cora had, no one wanted to touch it. Maybe a bartender like Tom Sedley or another outsider like Madeline Edgeworth, but not the common run of merchants, married folk, or working men. They would talk to someone who had a clandestine affair or had been through a divorce, but they didn't talk about those things. Taboo. Blacklisted.

So a fellow went it alone. Someone said how are you? and he said fine. There was no point in saying, "I went dead inside. I loved a woman and we got forced apart. Had some shame tangled in there. Felt like a curse from the gods. Let me tell you how it happened." No, not at all. He might as well tell them his guts were falling out of his ass and he had boils on his peter. Few people took an interest in those kinds of maladies.

At least he was working. Earning a dollar a day, getting some muscle. That was better than moping in his room. The first month, when he hit the wall, had been the worst. He had all the time in the world and was too paralyzed to do anything about it. It seemed like too much, too big a heap or lump, to stab or hack at. Now he took it a little at a time, each task like a piece of ditch to be cleaned, each day another notch on the stick. Work with a crowd of men, three men, two men, one, but when it came to the hard work, always alone. That was all right. He knew how.

Lane rode into town with Nick and Elbert when spring roundup was through. July had come around with hot weather, and dust rose from the horse hooves.

"Ah learned my lesson laist year," said Elbert. "Ah come into town and wanted to cut it wide open and do ever'thin' at once. This time Ah'm gonna take it slower. Start with a barbershop shave. How 'bout you-all?"

Nick, who shaved himself every two or three days, said he might, but not right away.

Lane ran his hand across his chin. The whiskers were long enough that he could pull them through the flat of two fingers. "I think I'll leave it," he said. "Might get a trim around the edges."

They rode on, Elbert chattering about what he planned to do and in what order. As they drew near to Willow Springs, Lane began to feel some of the old apprehension. His stomach went queasy, and a restlessness came into his arms and legs. No matter; he'd face what he had to, if it was only the ghosts.

Elbert went to the barbershop, and Nick said he had a place to go on his own. Lane figured it had something to do with girls, and not being in the market for that quite yet, he went to the Last Chance Saloon.

Tom Sedley put a mug of beer in front of him. "Didn't recognize you at first, but you don't look too bad. A couple of gray spots, but better than the last time I saw you. Where you been?"

"Workin' for Nance Fredman, out on the Rosette Ranch." He drank from the mug and savored the taste.

"Oh, yeh. Hardly ever see him anymore. The work agree with you?"

"Seems to. Like Nance says, gettin' windburned and sleepin' on the ground does a fellow some good."

"I thought you left completely. Then I heard you were out there somewhere, but I wasn't sure where."

"Well, that's the place. I didn't have anywhere else to go, and I thought I'd stay around this area." He took another drink. "Any news?"

"Not along the lines you're probably thinkin' of. You know he sold that new house to Joseph Saxton."

"That was in the works. I tried to imagine the two of them working out a deal."

"I think they did all right when they made the deal, but then what's-his-name came back with some extra charges, and it cost a few hundred more than expected."

"So he left town about the way we might have imagined."

"I'd say. Your ex-employer had a small disillusionment as well. Got left stiff for the amount of a couple of shipments of lumber."

"Too bad."

"Uh-huh. He might get paid yet, who knows when, but in the meanwhile he's like the little puppy in the joke."

"I'm not sure I know that one."

"Oh. Well, it goes like this. A man's walkin' downtown, and he sees another fella sellin' puppies. Cute little black puppies. The man asks what kind they are, and the fella says they're Republican puppies, cost fifty cents apiece. The man says, 'Huh,' and goes on. A few days later he sees the same fella, and this time he tells 'im they're Democrat puppies and cost six bits. 'Well, what the hell?' he says. 'Just last week you told me they were Republican puppies.' 'They were,' says the other fella, 'but now they've got their eyes open.' "

Lane laughed. "I haven't heard that one before."

"You can tell it either way, have 'em Republicans first, or Democrats, or whatever you want."

"Sure. But the idea's funny." Lane took a drink of his beer. "There was another person I was interested in knowing about. You remember the fellow I pummeled so mercilessly out here on the sidewalk?"

"I remember it perfectly."

"Do you know what he's up to?"

"He's got the blacksmith shop here in town."

"The hell he does. I saw him twenty miles out on the range, and he said he was working for some outfit there. Said I'd see him during the roundup. Well, I expected to see him at every chuck wagon, in every camp—not that I was looking forward to it, mind you—and he never showed."

"I think he did go to work for someone out there for a little while, doin' blacksmith work, but then Buxton keeled over one day at the forge. So Collier saw the opportunity, came back into town, and took it over."

"Huh. I wonder what he was doing out on the range anyway. But at least I don't have to be looking for him over my shoulder out there anymore. You'd think people could let things rest."

Sedley gave him a wry smile. "Do you?"

"I don't have any hard feelings. But the other kind, no, I can't say I'm done with all of that. If someone had let the thing die of its own accord, it would be different. But I still think about it all."

Sedley shook his head. "Jeez, after all the misery she put you through, and a thrashin' on top of it."

"Ah, hell, Tom. She didn't do any of that to me. She couldn't help the way things turned out."

The barkeep laughed. "You're all right, Lane. You're from the old school, aren't you? Nothing is ever a lady's fault."

"I guess so. I hadn't thought about it that way, but I suppose that's a difference between me and someone else, who took it all as if it happened only to him." He looked at Sedley, who was shaking his head in good nature now. "I can tell what you're thinking. I'm like that little puppy that hasn't got his eyes opened yet."

"Ah, you're all right. I'm glad to see you didn't get it beat out of you."

Chapter Eight

Lane stood outside the Northern Star Saloon as a woman's voice carried through the air. He recognized the song as "Cowboy Jack," a sentimental song in the style of an old mountain ballad. Two lovers quarrel and separate until the cowboy, out on the range, decides to come back. When he does, he learns that his girl has died. His friends tell him:

Your sweetheart waits for you, Jack,
Your sweetheart waits for you,
Out on the lonely prairie,
Where the skies are always blue.

The song chilled him as he stood in the autumn night; it was the first woman's voice he had heard in months.

This town of Lusk had some bustle to it at the moment. Fall roundup was through, and most outfits had shipped their beef. Elbert had left for Tennessee as soon as the steers were in the pens, and after the animals were loaded, Nick and the old man drove the extra horses back to the ranch. Lane was on his own for a while.

He stood on the sidewalk, waiting for another song and watching the men come and go. So many of them seemed to be going somewhere with a purpose, even when they turned into a saloon or a dry goods store.

Something familiar struck him about a man who rode up to the hitch rack, dismounted, and tied his horse. The man stepped onto the sidewalk and thumped his way to the open door of the Northern Star. He stood there for a moment before going in, and as the light fell on his features, Lane placed him. He was the man who had come into St. John's office looking for the Umo Ranch. Two seasons of work in this country had brought him up in the world; he was wearing clean clothes, a hat in good condition, and a new sheepskin coat. Lane noted the boots. They were scuffed on top like a range rider's, and they had spurs strapped on.

It occurred to Lane that he could buy a pair of spurs for himself in this town. To a shopkeeper he would be just another man come in off the range, not the ex-friend of the merchant's wife who had had a short-lived literary society.

Lane found a mercantile store that carried a good supply of cinches, latigos, quirts, bridles, bits, and spurs, as well as a few saddles. Some of the spurs were ornate, with braided designs inlaid or etched. One pair had an eye-catching design. Lane picked up a single spur and saw that its shank had the form of a woman's leg. The metal looked like polished silver with a gold garter. Nice shape. He set the spur down and picked a plainer style with rowels about the size of a nickel. The storekeeper came over.

"Find a pair you like?"

"I think these will be fine."

"You want a pair of leathers?"

"How's that?"

"Leathers. To strap 'em on."

"Oh, of course. Let's see what you've got."

"A lot of the punchers use these with the buckles."

"What's the difference between them and the others?"

"These cost thirty-five cents more, but they're handier."

"That should be pretty good, then."

Lane paid the man and walked out with his purchase. He had a good idea how he could learn to put these things together.

Nick sat on the bunk opposite Lane's. "Those look pretty good," he said. "Buckles to the outside. You want that spur to ride up and down a little but not too much. If you haven't worn a pair before, you might take a turn or two around the yard before you go into town to show 'em off, like Elbert did, and trip over 'em and fall on the sidewalk."

With a few turns around the yard, he saw what Nick meant. He gouged his left boot a couple of times, and he almost tripped himself once.

"And you need to remember to take 'em off if you plan to do any sneakin'."

"What kind would I be doin'?"

"Oh, deer, for instance."

Lane walked along the creek bottom, dry now and full of color. A week since first frost, the chokecherry bushes were turning. Some were all of a color—pink, red, or yellow—and some had a mix. The wild plum leaves varied from pink to yellow. The larger trees, the box elder and cottonwood, were turning yellow and dropping leaves.

First frost was more dramatic than last frost because a person knew when it had taken place. With last frost, he went on for a while, looked back, and figured that had been it. Maybe that was the way things had to be with Cora—in the past for a while before he would realize they were over. He still didn't think they were, but he wondered if he thought so by himself. Last night he had dreamed of big black cherries on a tree, some as big as plums but still round—a full month since any of these trees had fruit. He wondered if she had dreams like that.

He walked slow, cradling the rifle in his arms. No hurry. Nance said he could stay at the bunkhouse as long as he wanted, just help out with chores. He felt useful. If he brought in a deer, he would be earning some of his keep.

Nice rifle. Lean and tight and capable. Good of Nick to lend it. Might get one like it. He raised it at a blur in the brush, then let it down.

He felt set for the winter ahead. Most of the season's wages were salted away in his wallet at the bottom of his duffel bag. He could buy a rifle and still go somewhere, do something for himself. Just not sure what, though.

The creek bed widened out, and the broadleaf trees and bushes gave way to willow brush. Lane poked along, casting his eye from one side to the other.

He stopped. Something in the brush didn't look like everything else. The willow branches were pale yellow and red, but these points were dull brown, light at the tips. He thought he could make out the form of a deer crouched in the brush, but he wasn't sure. Nick's tutelage came to him. Be sure of your target, don't shoot at a rustle in the bushes; give an animal a chance to stand up.

Lane stood motionless for a long minute or more, and the tips didn't move. Then he stepped forward and the deer rose crashing out of the willows. The antlers moved up and down as the buck bounded three times, then snapped to the left, showing his pale rump. Nick's advice came again; don't shoot him in the ass. Lane raised the rifle and tried to pick up the animal in the sights as it went up the hill. He hoped the deer would stop and look around, as he had seen more than once with Nick. But it didn't stop. It charged over the hill and was gone.

Lane's heart was beating fast as he lowered the rifle. It all happened so quick, and he didn't have a chance. Shouldn't have shot anyway. Did the right thing. Hell of a big deer. Antlers held up like a cradle as he went over the hill. That was the way things went, though.

Nance said it was time to pay a visit to old Guy Page. He gave Nick a winter coat that was frayed on the cuffs but still had a good wool liner.

"Take him this, and a quarter of beef."

On the way out of the ranch, Lane asked about the man they were going to visit.

"Old Guy Page. He lives way the hell and gone out there. He's got hardly any of his own cattle anymore. Nance sends him some beef two or three times every winter."

"Are they old friends?"

"Not really. Nance just doesn't want him killin' any Rosette cattle or strainin' himself if he kills someone else's."

When they got to Guy Page's place, which was a run-down little set of buildings in what looked like prime rattlesnake country, the old man met them at the door. He had a wizened face, washed-out blue eyes, and a sweat-stained old hat that looked as if he slept in it. He walked bent over, and his belt rode halfway up to his chest. After showing the boys where to hang the meat in his lean-to, he made them sit down in the kitchen.

Right away he started quizzing Lane on where he came from and how he came to be staying on with old Nance.

Lane answered that he had lived out here for a couple of years, had worked for Wilson St. John for a while, and then gone to work for Nance.

"St. John, huh? Well, he's a fine one. How was he to work for? Fine, I bet. The son of a bitch. Buys up land where good men went broke because of the likes of him and others. Skullduggery. Mucky-mucks. Seen how the railroads done it, and now they do it theirselves. What kind of work did you do?"

"I worked in his office."

"And why'd you turn to nursemaidin' cows?"

"He let me go."

"What for? For bein' too honest? Ha-ha. Don't worry, though. If you did get fired for that, you wouldn't be the first. Or the last neither, I'm thinkin'."

"The main reason he let me go was that one of his friends had something against me. Nothing to do with my work."

"One of his friends, huh? Well, he's got plenty. And every one of 'em'll have a better coffin than you or me. But you know what?"

"What?"

"No one beats the devil. Not in the end. That's the one fair thing about this life. Some go out smellin' better'n others, but no one beats it."

The old man went on for a while longer. He told how he had seen the Indians get pushed out, the railroads and barbed wire come in; he had seen the big foreign investors and the little sodbusters come and go. Most of all he hated the mucky-mucks. "The worst thing that ever happened to this country since I been here was the bad winter of '86 to '87, and the best thing would be to have another one just like it. It would be just the thing for some of these sons of bitches. Send 'em packin', and let some honest men get it back." Then when he seemed to have talked himself out enough, he told the boys he didn't want to keep them late and get them in trouble with the boss. "And send my thanks to old Nance. Tell him I hope he's all right and doesn't die any time soon."

Back out on the trail, Lane remarked to Nick that old Guy was quite a character.

"He sure is," said Nick. "But you know, if Nance lives long enough, he'll turn out to be quite a bit like him."

A light snow lay on the ground as Lane rode out of the ranch yard. The rifle scabbard under the stirrup fender would take some getting used to, but he felt equipped. Horse and rifle, spurs, gloves, knife. Nick and the old man both said it was good to hunt deer after a snow.

First he walked the creek bottom where he had seen the big one a few days earlier. Finding nothing, he rode farther west, in the direction of Squaw Rock. Halfway there he cut north toward a set of breaks where Nick suggested he look for deer.

At the head of the breaks he tied the horse to a slender pine, then pulled out the rifle and went on his hunt. He followed a ridge where it sloped down to the north. Pine trees were scattered across this ridge and the two on either side, until the ridges smoothed out into a grassy valley. Nothing taller than knee-high brush grew on the plain, and he could see at least a mile as the country spread out for a hundred eighty degrees to the north. He saw no animals at all.

He worked his way back up the ridge to the area where the pine trees ended. Snow still lay in some of the shadowed spots, while it had all melted on the grassland. He thought he should hunt across the ridges, looking into the next draw as he came to the top of each one. Undecided on which way to go, he chose west so as not to have the sun in his eyes. He went down into the draw, crossed over, and climbed onto the next ridge. The view looked the same as before, with yet another ridge beyond. He turned around and studied the way he came, so he would know his way back. The number of draws changed, as some of them ran into others. He had learned that lesson on foot already, from down below. Shading his eyes with his hand at his hat brim, he picked out a landmark, a tall dead snag of a pine tree. It stood at the head of the ridge beyond the one he came down. With that detail fixed in his mind, he went down into the next draw and continued west.

One ridge, two—the climbs were getting steeper. He remembered to take it slow so he wouldn't be heaving in deep breaths when he came to a crest and saw something. With each slope he took the last few steps soft and separate, letting his eyesight clear the rim little by little. When the second of these two draws came into full view and revealed nothing, he went down and up for one more.

Now he saw a white clay bluff, some eight or ten feet tall, sticking out of the side of the next ridge. A few yards to the right of the base, in good position to take in the morning sun, a blacktail buck was grazing. Lane's heart thumped and he sank back, closing the deer out of view.

He took off his gloves and put them away, then eased a shell into the chamber. Crawling to the top again, he placed the deer before bringing the rifle around. The animal had taken a few steps. The big antlers moved as the deer turned its head to graze and then took another step.

Lane eased the rifle upward and shifted into shooting position. The movement must have caught the buck's eye, for his branched head came up and he started trotting. Lane followed in the sights until the deer stopped and turned. Now. The rifle crashed and the deer went down, front quarters first. Dust stirred, and then the animal was still.

Lane's heart was pounding and his mouth was dry. He knew he had done something big. He had crossed over, pulling the trigger and sending a bullet he couldn't take back. He had brought down a wild animal larger than himself.

Now he watched to see if the deer would move. When he was sure it was not going to rise, he went down the slope and up the other side of the draw. His mind was still absorbing what had happened in those suspended few seconds when he pulled the trigger and the deer went down. He had done nothing wrong; to the contrary, he had succeeded at what he set out to do. But he had a full sense of the magnitude of his act. Alone in a vast land, he had done something that could not be changed.

Lane went to the door of the shack and looked out at the whiteness. A few inches had fallen in the night. According to his notch stick, it was the first of December. Nothing to worry about. Nance said if the snow got a foot deep to come back to the ranch. Both horses knew the way, day or night, and the packhorse would have a lighter load than when he went out.

Lane closed the door and glanced at his stack of firewood. Good thing he had gotten in a pile of it the day before. Not bad. A month's wages to hang out at a cow camp and keep an eye peeled for strange doin's, as Nance put it. Nothing more. Just ride out once a day and take a look. Ride one horse one day, the other the next. The rest of the time, he could try to keep the shack warm enough that the canned tomatoes didn't freeze.

Sometimes it seemed like the last outpost. Not only was he cut off from whoever might be called his people, which he had been since he came to the West, but he was also cut off from the things that gave him his bearings—his books, which were still packed away with Rox Barlow, and the antlers, which were hooked over a beam to dry in the bunkhouse. Here he had his own jackknife. Even the buffalo coat and the rifle were on loan from Nance.

Not bad, all alone. He could leave the door of the sheet-iron stove open and watch the coals. Think about what it all meant. In the novels it was like a double life—the everyday world of work and obligation, and the other world of risk and adventure. Secret love affairs were governed by a clear sense of purpose—desire and achievement. He told himself that his and Cora's hadn't been that way. It was real. Love flowing both ways with no control—a giving over of himself, a complete vulnerability that led him to moments of despair.

The desperation was not so strong now, though he still felt he was in the lone winter he had written about before he threw away his treatise. Now he wished he had kept it. At the least he could see how far he had come. With time and distance, he felt calmer about the whole ordeal. He wasn't pulled into treacherous uncertainty, day in and day out.

Nevertheless, he hadn't put it behind him. He could see that. He went over it all the time. He still marveled at what had seemed so real; almost with a sense of incredulity, he recalled those intimate moments when he had access to it all—his lips on her breast, his hand on her buttock—easy and natural and unrestrained. Then it was all locked away, so that it seemed almost unreal. Almost. But it had been there.

He didn't think it did any harm to remember those things. He was not making himself feel the way he did in those first few wretched days and weeks when he hit the wall. Even when he went out on his ride and, catching first sight of the shack when he came over the ridge, fancied that she would be waiting there, he did not feel he was punishing himself. But of course the shack was always empty, and he cooked his camp meat alone.

He opened the door of the stove and stuck in a length of pine. A man didn't need much. He could get by.

Lane asked Nance if he could borrow the same two horses for a trip of his own. One to ride and one to pack his bed and camp. He said he wanted to go out and see a few things and didn't want to go through a medley of coaches and rented horses. Nance said fine, if he got himself froze to death the two horses could find their way home. And besides, they both had his brand on them.

After a cold camp out in the open, he continued south the next day. He came to a pine ridge, followed the trail as it wound through, and rode into Hartville. Nance's words came to him. "Don't stop there unless you have to, boy. They'll skin ya." He stayed on the trail until he came out of the hills on the other side, at nightfall. The Platte Valley lay below him.

The next day he followed the old Oregon Trail and made it almost to Nebraska. He camped near a place called Cold Springs. The following day, he crossed into Nebraska and went past Scotts Bluff rising from the hill on his left. When he camped that evening, he could see the lights of Gering in the valley below.

As he rode into the town the next morning, he began to doubt for the first time the wisdom of his journey. His abdomen tensed with nerves, and a pain was stabbing him down inside where he had felt the fire that would not go away. He didn't expect to see Cora, not any more than he did the last time he went past her empty house in Willow Springs. But he was in her country now, and McGee's as well. Somewhere around here he had done some of his deeds—taken Cora's maidenhood, taken someone else's property with or without a legal signature, sold things he didn't have a title to. Worse than not feeling a kinship with the place, Lane felt the presence of earlier things gone wrong.

In Gering he stopped at a stable and asked the way to Cedar Canyon. The stable man asked him if he was looking for someone in particular, and he said no. He planned to make this as trackless an excursion as he could, so he said he just wanted to see the place, as he had heard it was pretty.

"Oh, it's all right. But the land's better here in the valley. You lookin' to take up land?"

"No, just see where other people did."

"Oh, you can find it all right. Just follow the trail south, and after a while you'll see where the canal comes in on the west. Keep an eye out for a road to the right that crosses the canal. If you don't do that and come to a place where the main trail crosses the canal, you'll be comin' to the Wildcat Hills and you'll know you went too far."

"Huh. The Wildcat Hills? There's some of those where I come from."

"Where's that?"

"Over in Wyoming, up toward the Niobrara."

"Nope. These are different ones."

Lane spent that day riding to Cedar Canyon and back. He didn't ask any questions or stop to talk to anybody. All he wanted was to see the hills and trees and rocks that Cora had seen so many times. When he had done that, he crossed the canal and went back to town to spend the night.

The return trip took four days, like the trip out. He pushed the horses less and did not camp in the same places, so he made it only as far as Willow Springs on the fourth night. He put up the horses and took a room in the hotel.

Before going to bed, he went out for a walk in the cold night. A layer of snow lay everywhere. It hadn't been swept or shoveled, and a three-quarter moon was out, which made for a bright night. He walked to the end of town, where her house still sat in darkness. He thought of the times he had seen her at the window, but everything was dark and closed up now. The moonlight, however, gave it a theatrical look, and he recalled an opera he had seen as a young boy. In it, a lovely woman in black stood singing in the night outside a prison tower, where a man stood at a barred window, also in shadow, and sang back to her.

The next day, he rode into the Rosette Ranch before noon. Nance was sitting in the bunkhouse kitchen slicing potatoes, and he hardly looked up when Lane walked in.

"Well, ten days on your own, and you made it back. Been to see the critter?"

"Of one kind or another."

"I looked out in the yard every mornin' and never seen the horses, so I figured you didn't fall off and die in a snowdrift. Of course, you could have froze to death when you had them tied out somewhere, and the crows would be pickin' at all three of yuh."

"Not this time. It would make a good story to warn other greenhorns, but I'm not dead yet."

"Just as well," said the old man. "Nick took off and won't be back for a month, and we're almost out of firewood. So go ahead and make yourself at home."

Lane crumpled a piece of paper and tossed it into the stove. He glanced at his books, set up in a crate he had tipped sideways. Just having them in the same room helped him write some of the stanzas, and he found help in reading poems for meter and rhyme. This was the third day of working on the poem—or song, really. He could hear the melody in his head, then write the metered verses to fit. He scratched and rewrote, shifted lines and parts of lines. Nance kept to himself in the kitchen or in his quarters on the other side, so Lane didn't feel as if he had someone looking over his shoulder. He hummed the melody, sang a verse under his breath, tinkered some more.

He thought he had it in pretty good shape now. He crumpled two more pieces of paper and tossed them into the stove, then held out the fair copy and admired it. Across the top, in larger letters than the rest, he read the title: "Song for Lone Winter."

These weren't little verses, and she might not even care for some of it, but he had gotten on paper what he needed.

When Nance went out back, Lane read it aloud to himself. His voice felt steady and strong.

Now the wild geese of winter cross over my sky,
And the sun slips in scarlet as I watch the day die.
I stand at the doorway and look down the lane,
Where the dark ruts in twilight are all that remain.

It's a cold world at nightfall as I step back inside,
Put a log on the embers where the fire has died,
Then return to the window to gaze out again
And remember the days that I waited in vain—

How the dreams died and withered, in the grip of despair,
A shroud on the heart without candle or prayer—
For the desperate in love have no right to complain
When there's ice on the doorstep and frost on the pane.

Now the fire grows stronger and I shake off the chill
That comes in the evening when all has gone still.
With the hearth fire and lamplight I once more regain
The warmth that fled from me as I whispered her name.

My blood's in December but it still has a trace
Of a pulse that once quickened in secret embrace,
And the blood can remember the fluting refrain
Of a meadowlark after a clean summer rain.

Through the long night of winter, alone on the plain,
I feel the warmth seep into marrow and vein,
A soft flush of hope, given out by the flame,
Though there's ice on the doorstep and frost on the
pane.

At the first break of morning I'll rise with the day
And gather my horses, the dun and the gray.
In a world dull as deerhide, the sun like a stain,
As the geese overhead stitch the sky with their skein,

I'll battle December with bridle and rein,
Forge one day to another like links in a chain.
If I fall from the saddle I will not complain
About ice on the doorstep and frost on the pane.

Nance came back into the kitchen and clanged around on the cookstove. "When do you think you'll be goin' into town again?" he asked.

"I don't know. Why?"

"It's been a while since we had any snakebite medicine. Good for cabin fever, too."

"I'll remember it next time I go." It was hard to tell what Nance had on his mind. "Are you fixin' to cook something?"

"I'm in a mood for a steak."

"You want me to cut a couple off that quarter?"

"Sure."

Lane went to the storeroom where a hindquarter of beef hung from a beam. He cut out two steaks and took them into the comparative warmth of the kitchen.

Nance adjusted the damper on the stove. "Were you talkin' to yourself when I was out back?"

"Not exactly. I was reading out loud. Something I wrote, and I wanted to hear it."

"You know, it sounded almost like a song."

"It's not far from one."

Nance shook his head. "Well, I guess they got to come from somewhere. And to think I took you for a bugologist."

Lane stood at the doorway of the dining room, looking at the tables and deciding where he wanted to sit. Only one table was occupied, and it was not out of the question. Madeline Edgeworth looked his way and gave him a signal to come over.

"Feel free to join me," she said, "unless you're expecting someone else."

"No, I'm not. Thanks." He pulled out a chair across from her and sat down.

"And how are you getting through the winter?" Her dark eyes, relaxed, put him at ease.

"Oh, all right. I've been out at the ranch most of the time. I came in today to pick up a few things."

"How is it for work? Do you get along with it?"

"I do. I've learned to do for myself in a lot of ways. You know, the basic things. Handle a horse, throw a rope, work with tools. Rustle up my own food, keep from freezing to death. Things you don't think about much until you have to."

"Self-reliance."

"Yes, and I don't mind saying, it's made me tougher."

"You look more rugged," she said, with an appraising eye. "In a handsome way. You look good in a beard."

"Thanks. But don't make me blush. The other cowboys might see it."

She gave a light laugh. "Well, I'm glad to see you're doing well. You do look better. You don't have as much of the haunted look as before."

"But I still have some?"

"Maybe a touch." She smiled. "But there aren't many things in this life that you can't get over."

"I've gotten that idea, but it's hard to make something happen."

"That's true. And it's not just a matter of waiting a specified amount of time. I remember thinking, ah, well, I'll wait one year. But things don't expire like a contract."

"I think if things had ended a little neater, I could have come to more of a conclusion. As it was, I felt I got to take plenty of the blame and didn't get to make any of the decision."

"That's a bad way."

"I'd say. She told me, just before it all came to a dead end, that he had a favorite phrase. 'What kind of a man? What kind of a man would do something like that?' And the looks I got from so many people around town said the same thing, as if she hadn't had a part in it." He had a strange feeling of comfort as he took in her eyes, her dark hair, her full bosom. "Maybe I'm talking too much."

"Not at all. I know what you mean, and it's so narrow-minded. If there's trouble in a marriage, it's not all the fault of just one person. And one person alone, from the outside, can't break up a marriage." She waved her hand at the town in general. "But try to tell some of these people."

"So that was one part, getting all the blame, or at least more than my share, when he didn't get any at all. And he pulled some things. The other part was in not having any voice. He went around and got to everybody first, got them to help wear her down, and gave her the idea that she had no choice. Told her he'd take the children and—oh, I know I'm going on too much. But once I got started—ah, to hell with him."

"Just be glad he's gone, even if he took her with him. He's a crooked son of a bitch, and if there's any justice in this world, someone he rooked will catch up with him on some dark night."

"That might be too much to hope for."

"Lane," she said, drawing out the moment, "you're a smart man. But smart men do foolish things."

"I know. We've talked about that before."

"I don't mean what you did in the past. I mean something you're still doing."

"What's that?"

"Hoping. If I were you, I wouldn't hope for anything. Not in that area."

As long as he had been able to talk about his problem, he felt uplifted. Now he felt a drop. "You're probably right. But it's hard to make myself think in some other way."

"Then don't try to make yourself think. Just *do* something else."

"Do? Do what?"

"Do something, silly. Fight fire with fire."

Their plates arrived, and he looked at the roast beef and gravy. Then he raised his eyes to meet hers. "I admit I'm kind of slow. But I haven't forgotten everything."

It was not frenzied passion, but it was not as detached as getting a shoe shine. For the short time he was with her, he knew what he had been missing. Now he was satisfied, his whole body undeprived. The magic of her breasts, the motion of her body—it was all more than a countermeasure. It was restorative in itself.

Tom Sedley put the mug of beer in front of him. "And how's our office clerk turned plainsman?"

"Still in the game, Tom."

Movement at the end of the bar caught his eye, and he saw Quist leaning on one elbow and taking a puff from his pipe. The fellow seemed to get around. He had come through the dining room when Lane and Madeline were finishing their meal, and here he was again.

Madeline in the dining room, full-breasted and

sparkling. Do something, silly. Well, he did, and he sure hadn't forgotten how. He was still in the game, but he hadn't been still with her. It was all good motion.

CHAPTER NINE

Lane rode into Willow Springs, his right hand tensed on the lead rope. On the sidewalk to his left, Collier in a smudged canvas coat was talking to Wilson St. John, nodding in the way men had of currying favor. Lane kept his eyes straight ahead until he was well past them; then he looked over his right shoulder to see how the pack was riding.

He rode past the saloon and the hotel, still not looking to either side. A block farther, he stopped in front of the low-slung building that stood by itself. The trader came to the doorway, holding a piece of dried meat to his mouth and raising his knife to slice off a bite.

"How do you do, Curley? The fur buyer is supposed to come today, isn't he?"

"Yup."

"Mind if I leave my horses here?"

"Fine with me."

Lane tied his horses and walked back toward the center of town. Nance wanted him to ask around for Guy Page, and he could do that while he was waiting to sell his pelts.

A voice stopped him. "Hello, Lane."

Wilson St. John had stopped outside his office. Collier was gone, presumably back to his blacksmith shop.

Lane returned the greeting. "Good morning."

"How are you getting by?"

"All right, thanks."

"Still working for Nance Fredman?"

"Well, I've been staying there. He hasn't had much work for me, but I've stayed at the bunkhouse both winters now."

"Oh, I see. I heard you took up a claim out in the breaks."

"I did. That's where I hunted some of my coyotes this winter. All the way from there over to Nance's place."

"That's good. I wish you well at it. At that, and everything else." He held out his hand.

Lane shook it. "Thanks."

St. John went into his office, and Lane continued walking down the sidewalk. Although the encounter had lasted less than a minute, it gave him something to reflect on. He didn't detect a note of apology in St. John, but there seemed to be a confirmation of no hard feelings. That was all right. St. John didn't have to go to the trouble, but he did. He might have been taken in a little at one time, but he didn't stay in business by keeping his eyes closed. And as Cora had said, McGee was a good talker. Now that St. John had a better view, he was doing what he thought was right.

Lane counted back. Two years since the catastrophe, three since he first met Cora. The passage of a couple of years amended some things, but time didn't heal all wounds. He still thought of Cora a hundred times a day.

Madeline had told him not to hope for anything, but as he walked down the sidewalk he could hear the song that carried on the air to him outside the Northern Star.

Your sweetheart waits for you, Jack,
Your sweetheart waits for you,
Out on the lonely prairie,
Where the skies are always blue.

He heard the part he wanted, which he knew wasn't the same as what happened in the song. The lovers quarreled, the girl died of love, and Jack went to make amends too late. Maybe Cora was dead, or dandling another baby and in love with her husband. He didn't think so. Even if she wasn't waiting for him, she had been taken away against her will, and she still thought of him. He knew that. But none of it did any good, and he still had to try to get over her.

Lane held his left hand against the sorrel's neck as he brushed with his right. After working with someone else's stock for two years, he could feel the difference when he brushed his own. These were good horses, the sorrel and the bay. No kicking or bucking, and he could pack on either of them. Nance wouldn't sell him the two he wanted, but he was getting used to these.

He didn't have much to show for two years—a pair of horses, saddle and gear, clothes for the range, a rifle, a few visits with Madeline for five dollars a tumble—but he was getting somewhere. And he hadn't been indentured, like Jacob and Laban and the seven-year switch. Of course, after seven years Jacob got something, even if it wasn't the woman he wanted.

Hair came off the horses in wads this time of year. Tufts of it lay all around. Lane rubbed hard against the shoulder, where the muscle rippled as dust and hair and tiny flakes came away.

When he was finished with both horses, he turned them into the pasture. Just in time. Heavy clouds had been rolling in, and now a slow, cold rain was starting to fall. Lane went to the stable and stood by the back door, where he could see the rain settling on the rangeland. The country had a mixed hue, with the first green appearing but the dry grass of winter still visible. The plains stretched away in every direction, moving through flatlands, hills, buttes, and breaks. As far as he could see, the country was taking in the slow rainfall. He could imagine the land receiving the rain, getting ready to put it to use. Black-root sod taking the message from the thin blades of grass. In some places, spread at liberal distances, trees were feeling the rain on their needles or emerging leaves, telling the roots.

The land was bigger than anyone. It had its surprises, but it didn't lie or cheat. It was lonesome country, but it didn't promise anything else. Now it was taking what it got, a good slow rain.

Nance seemed to be worried about Guy Page, but he didn't want to send the boys out.

"You just took him some meat a month ago, so if you just drop in, he'll think I think he can't take care of himself. I don't want that. But, Lane, when you go into town, ask in a couple of places."

"I asked in the barbershop last time."

"Oh, they think they know everything in there, and if it happens right outside their window, they do. Ask in the post office. Daniels knows everything that comes and goes in the ranch country."

Daniels said he had sent a letter from Kansas out that way about ten days earlier, and he supposed word would have come back if the old man hadn't been there to take it.

Lane thanked him and turned to walk out. As he did, he saw a woman coming in. He stepped aside and smiled. She smiled back. Nice-looking woman. Clean blond hair, bright eyes, figure still held together. Any woman who smiled at him in this town was all right in his book. He lingered a second; then, seeing no point in it, he headed for the door.

The postmaster's voice stopped him. "This man right here can help you."

Lane turned and saw the woman poised with an envelope in her hand.

Daniels spoke again. "This lady wants to send a letter to Nick Robison. He's out at the ranch, isn't he?"

"He sure is."

The postmaster spoke to the woman. "I'd send it with him anyway. If you want, you can save the postage."

"Thank you. I can do that."

Lane took a couple of steps toward her. "I'll be glad to carry a letter," he said. "I'll be going back out in a little while."

She thanked Daniels a second time and stepped away from the window. "I appreciate it," she said, handing the envelope to Lane. "It's from my niece, and I'm sure he'll be happy to get it."

"The sooner the better." Lane smiled as he took the letter. "By the way, my name's Lane Weller."

She did not stiffen or cringe, but rather held out her hand. "I'm Lydia Desmond."

He took her hand. "Pleased to meet you." He stood aside to let her go out the door, then joined her on the sidewalk. "Going this way?"

"Yes."

"Mind if I walk along?"

"No, not at all."

"Are you new in town, Miss Desmond?"

"Mrs."

"Oh, yes."

She seemed to hesitate and then said, "Yes, I'm

new here. I've moved into town after being out on the ranch for several years."

"Oh. And does you husband like it better in town?"

"He liked it on the ranch, but he had to give it up." She paused. "He's buried there."

"I'm sorry to hear that."

"It was not a surprise. He was ill for a long time. And he was not very old. Well, a few years older than me, but still young for a man."

"I should say so." He didn't speak for a few seconds, and when she didn't either, he resumed. "You've moved into town, then?"

"Yes. I've sold the ranch, and I've bought a house here in Willow Springs."

Lane felt a tightening in his stomach. "You'll miss the open country, unless you're on the edge of town."

"I'm not. I took the little house that the blacksmith and his family used to have."

"Oh, yes. I know the one. I was sorry to hear about him."

"Yes, he was not so old, either." They stepped into the street to cross to the next block. "And yourself, Mr. Weller? Do you work on the same ranch as Nick Robison—that is, when you're not carrying the mail?"

"I've been working there, but I'm planning to make a change. I've taken up some land of my own—not much, just a quarter section—and I plan to go stay there for a while. Make some improvements. Keep things simple."

"Far from the madding crowd. I try to keep my life free from complications, too."

"It's the best way, when you can manage."

She paused in front of the butcher shop. "Well, I've got to go in here."

"Good enough. It's been nice meeting you."

"All the same. And thank you for delivering the letter."

"My pleasure, I assure you. Maybe we'll meet again the next time I'm in town."

"Perhaps." She gave him her hand again. This time he noticed how smooth it was. She hadn't been chopping wood or digging spuds.

Lane said very little when he handed the letter to Nick, but he did mention it had come to him through the aunt.

"Oh, Lydia. She's in town now."

Later that evening, Nick asked him when he was going to town again. Lane said any time, he wasn't on the payroll, and he was going to his own place as soon as they got the horses in. Nick said he would like to send a letter, and Lane answered that he'd be glad to deliver it and could save him the postage. Nick smiled.

Lydia opened the door at his knocking. The smell of baked bread wafted out around her, and she had apparently just taken off the apron that she held in her hand. She had her hair pinned up in coils as before, but she wasn't wearing a sweater, so he saw her figure to more advantage. She had a pert bosom and a trim waist.

"Mr. Weller. What a surprise!"

He held the letter between them. "The young man wanted to reply as soon as possible."

She laughed. "Of course."

He lingered. "I guess I'll be going."

"Very well. I would invite you in, but I don't have any coffee made. I've just finished baking, and my kitchen's in a mess."

"That's quite all right. Maybe another time."

"Yes. Don't be afraid to come by again."

"I won't." As he walked to his horse, he regretted the small lie. She would mention his name to someone, and that would be the end.

Elbert came back to the ranch with an ivory-handled pistol and a new pair of boots. He was sporting a mustache now, and Lane noticed he had two teeth missing on the left side, where before he had space for one.

At supper, the kid was all questions about the widder and her niece.

"Don't you mind," said Nance.

"Well, where's that leave me?"

"Just like before. Playin' a lone hand in the dark."

"No, I mean what if they both leave?" He waved his knife at Lane and Nick.

"Lane's goin' anyway. And whether Nick goes or stays, that don't change nothin'. There's still horses to ride and cattle to work." Nance cut off a chunk of steak. "There's no need to sulk. If you want some titty, go find you some. If you think you want a raise, remember Nick was here five years before I bumped him two bits."

Elbert chewed his meat on the right side. "I'm not sulkin'. And we'll see how good of a hand I can be."

"That's fine," said Nance. "That's all we care about."

From his place on the sofa, Lane admired Lydia's hair in the lamplight. It hung loose at her shoulders, and he thought it looked darker than it did when it was put up.

"More coffee, Mr. Weller?"

"A little. And I wouldn't mind it if you called me Lane."

"Very well. You can call me by my first name, then."

"Lydia. It's a pretty name."

"Just don't call me Lydia Languish."

"Oh, from the play."

"Yes. One of the boys in school called me that, and he knew it made me angry."

He tipped his head. "I can't imagine you not having complete repose."

She put on a coy smile. "It's very rare. But it can happen. And you?"

"I'm not very hot-tempered. I think I tend to sit on things."

"The pensive type."

"You could say that."

"Then staying out on your own place might agree with you."

"Oh, I'm not a hermit, though. I like company."

She smiled more broadly now. "Do you expect to have much, out there?"

"Not unless I count Elbert, a kid that works on the ranch. He threatens to come over and see if I've broken my neck or fallen on a snake."

"You seem to be the careful type."

He thought she might be fishing for something. "I might disappoint him. I'm not a daredevil. And I'm probably more careful than I used to be."

"That's a good way to be. It helps keep things from getting complicated."

"I suppose so. But if you take the caution too far, people like Nick and Julie wouldn't ever do anything but hold hands."

Her chin raised a little. "Well, I don't think they've put the cart before the horse. They're getting married because they want to."

"Oh, I didn't mean anything different. But even that's a risk. If a person gets married, I suppose he—or she—puts everything on the line. And that can make things complicated."

"That's true. I'm sure we've both seen marriages that were miserable. But that doesn't mean a young couple shouldn't have hope."

"I agree. I believe in it entirely. Love, hope—the illusion, if it's that."

"You sound a bit cynical for one who has never been married."

She must have talked to someone, to know that much. "I attribute it to age," he said. "But I believe in love and its promises."

"You have a good way with words."

"I rehearsed it all before I came here."

They both laughed, and he knew he was not going to kiss her that night.

Walking out into the evening a little later, he thought he might have a beer in the Last Chance before going to the ranch. But when he saw Quist standing on the corner of the main street smoking his pipe, he lost his taste for it and went to the stable for his horse.

The coals gave off a strong, dry heat that mixed well with the aroma of roasting beef. Lane poked at the fire, then gave the spit a quarter turn. The meat was searing well all the way around.

Happy voices came from within the meeting hall. From time to time one of the wedding guests came outside and took a look, but the overcast weather kept most of them inside. Dressed in their best and congregating as a group, they seemed to have a communal personality, all of them on the traditional path of people who did things the usual way—work, maintain a household, follow the rules of normal conjugal relations. Some of them, like Lydia, who had turned out fine for the occasion, were not in a marriage at present; others, like Nance, gave it a nod of acquaintance as he passed it by; and the young single people, Elbert among them, no doubt wondered how and when it might come their way. But by appearances, at least, they were a harmonious group, dressed up and brought together to support the social order. In Lane's observation, there wasn't a renegade among them, while he, the one outside, was dressed in his working clothes and soaking up smoke.

Nick was getting married, going off on his own to start a new phase in his life. As the ranch hands said, when a man got married he quit punchin' cows. Maybe he got a foreman's job, with a little house, but he had to give up being a range cowboy, gone for weeks at a time and liable to break his neck any day. So Nick was leaving the Rosette, going to work for Julie's folks, where he could come back to the home corral every evening.

Lane dragged the shovel blade across the coals to bring out more of the redness. Nick was getting married. Elbert had a mustache. Nance was on his way to being like Guy Page. Maybe they all were. Lane knew one thing for sure. He wasn't on his way to being a young newlywed with most of his life ahead of him. Life was passing him by. He needed to do something, but he wasn't sure what.

One thing he wasn't going to do. He wasn't going to stick around and be Elbert's subordinate. He had all too clear an image of that young man earlier in the day, in necktie and starched shirt, looking over Lane's work at the barbecue.

"Well," he said, "it looks like Ah'm gonna be Nance's right-hand man."

Lane held his tongue. He imagined Nance would find someone to take Nick's place, and he might have someone in mind already. That would be for Elbert to find out. For his own part, he would be rolling up his gear when he got back to the ranch.

Lane squatted by the circle of rocks in front of his tent. The fire of small branches was catching on, lifting in thin orange flames and sending up wisps of smoke. He pushed at a couple of unburned ends, then laid the stick aside.

She had written more letters than he remembered. Until today he had kept them packed away in a pasteboard box with other papers, a box he had not untied when he took it to the ranch and now here.

The poetic way to do this, he told himself, would be to read them one by one as he burned them, but he did not want to relive what he was trying to get over. By another way of thinking, all of these letters, plus the ones the nemesis had burned, would all still be in existence in some ideal, philosophical plane. None of what he had shared with Cora could be undone; he just didn't need to go through it again.

He almost saved one note. It was a small half page, folded, not in an envelope. He had found it in his coat pocket after their last visit at Mrs. Canby's. It said simply *Dear Lane—Thank you for the loan of so much. It was real. Love, Cora.* He held it for a moment, his hand trembling, until he tossed it onto the fire. The updraft lifted it, and the crossbreeze deposited it against the inside of the rock border. He reached with the stick and dragged the slip of paper into the fire.

In a way, they were his words coming back to him. He had written in his letters and had told her in person that he often felt like something that had to be hidden, something to lie about, which went against his deeper feeling that their love was real and he wished they could show it to the world. And here she had said it was real. Maybe it was, but if that was the whole answer, things would have taken a much different direction.

Lane combed his hair one more time and brushed at the wrinkles in his shirt. Except for a few gray hairs, he didn't mind what he saw in the mirror. It was worth the expense of a night in the hotel to be able to take a hot bath and change into clean clothes. Lydia would notice his spruced-up look as well as the clean but unpressed shirt, and he hoped she would take it as a compliment.

She answered the door as usual and invited him in. "Thank you for the note," she said.

"I didn't want to drop in without warning."

"I'm glad you made it into town. How are things out at the breaks?"

"Normal, I think."

"That's good. Won't you sit down? I can offer you a slice of pie if you'd like."

"That sounds magnificent. I have to admit, I've been on a pretty basic diet."

"That's life on the range. My husband used to say, 'Rancher lean and farmer fat.' He said the farmers never got so far away from the kitchen that they couldn't put on a good feed at noon dinner. I saw it myself when I was growing up. Even during harvest, the women brought out big pots of hot food."

"It didn't get to you, though," he said with a wink.

She smiled. "Not yet. That's why I like company, so I don't end up eating the whole pie myself."

As she walked to the kitchen, he appreciated her comments. She was all of his age, getting closer to forty than thirty-five, and she hadn't started to spread out yet. Not having had any children would have had something to do with it, but she also practiced self-control. She liked to bake, but she wasn't the type to slather a big hunk of bread with a quarter pound of butter.

She came from the kitchen carrying a tray with two cups and one plate. She had cut him a generous piece of pie, and as she set down the tray and nudged the plate toward him, she said, "I had some earlier. Please enjoy it."

He imagined she had limited herself to a sliver, but he did not let himself feel guilty. "Thank you," he said. "It looks like apple."

"It is."

She sat with her hands folded as he ate the pie. In apparent reference to their last meeting, she said, "I haven't heard anything from Julie yet, but I'm sure she and Nick are doing fine."

"Oh, I'm sure."

"It was a very nice wedding. I didn't know you could cook."

"I can keep the meat from burning. But when it comes to finer things, like making a pie, I haven't gotten that far."

"It's not that much of a mystery."

"Oh, I know. Bunkhouse and chuck wagon cooks haze 'em, as they say. I'm sure I could learn it." He reflected. "Of course, it's a little more special when it comes from someone else's kitchen."

"Thank you. I think most men appreciate it. Until they get married. Then they expect it."

"Farmers."

She laughed. "I suppose so." Her hands moved in her lap. "And I suppose that's your way of saying you don't take anything for granted."

"Me? Not at all. Quite to the contrary, I'd say. If anything good happens to me, I take a little while to see there hasn't been a mistake."

"Oh, you're so cautious. But what I meant was, you keep your life pared down to what you can do for yourself."

"I suppose I've grown into that sort of habit."

"I would expect you're reserved in other ways as well. I would think you don't cross over into someone else's—territory, I guess—and expect things."

He frowned. "No reason to. I don't think it would occur to me."

Her hands folded again. "Well, men are men. And some of them, when they know a woman's been married—"

"Oh."

"Not all women are the same."

"Oh, I don't make any assumptions."

"That's good." She let out a breath, which he took as a sigh of relief. She must have heard something and wanted to make sure he didn't expect to put the cart before the horse. Even if she put a little fire in his chimney, he could measure his distance.

"I do think I'd like to try my hand at making a pie, though. Would it be much trouble for you to write out the recipe?"

"Oh, none at all. You can start out with fresh or dried apples, either one, you know. And the other things, like flour and salt and sugar and cinnamon, are all easy to get." She gave him a serious look. "Where do you think you'll bake it?"

"Oh, out at my place. I've got a Dutch oven. If I scorch the first one or two beyond hope, I can throw 'em out, and nobody'll be the wiser."

With a bit of a chill in the air, he decided to take a shortcut to his room. Out of habit he turned into an alley that led to the back door of the hotel. Not thinking about much else except the prospect of kissing Lydia on some future occasion and perhaps pressing her bosom against him, he was taken by surprise when Quist stepped out of the shadows and stood in front of him. Slight and hunched, the man had a menacing air as he held his hands by his side.

"Where do you think you're going?"

"I don't see where that concerns you."

"Maybe it does. I see you've been bothering decent women again."

"If you weren't snooping around spying on 'em,

you wouldn't notice so much. You could try minding your own business."

Collier's voice came up behind him, sending a shiver through his spine and shoulders. "You could try the same."

Lane turned around in time to catch a glancing blow off his temple. As he tried to raise his fists, he felt Quist pulling on him from behind. Collier punched him twice in the face and twice in the stomach. Lane pushed away from Quist and tried to swing at Collier, and then his feet went out from under him. Quist kicked him in the arm and then the ribs as Collier stood above him, fists clenched.

"Just a small reminder of what I told you before. Men get hurt much worse than this."

"So what have I got here, the hired bully teaming up with the Peeping Tom?"

"You've got this," said Quist, kicking him in the head.

In his room, Lane examined the damage. The last kick by Quist had left him with a swollen face and a black eye on the right side, but he had plenty of small bumps and scrapes elsewhere on his head as well. He took off his shirt, dirty now, and saw the bruise on his upper arm.

So Collier was still on the job. That meant something. Either McGee held a grudge for a long time or wasn't getting things his way enough to let things rest. And Quist getting in a few of his own. Why didn't he stay at home with his pasty wife instead of going around sniffing after other women?

He and Collier both, looking for a chance to punish someone else for doing what they'd like to try. To hell with them. He would remember this.

Then Collier's reminder of that earlier taunt. Men got killed for doing what he did. Maybe so, but McGee didn't have it in him to do it himself, and if he was going to have it hired he would have done it long ago. But it was more his style to put all the pressure on the woman and then hire out a beating or two.

Lane touched the bruise on his cheekbone. It was a similar kind of cowardice to that of men who worked on a higher level, men whose company McGee aspired to. They hanged a woman and brought in hired killers to take care of their list of undesirables.

Kill a man. Lane wondered if it would ever be his destiny to kill someone. Strange thought. He could think of killing McGee easier than he could think of killing a person in general. He doubted it would ever come to that. But he would remember the drubbing he got tonight. It wasn't the one he said he would take, and he had even burned that letter.

Chapter Ten

Lane jabbed at the hillside with his shovel. A fellow could live in a dugout for a year, he figured. In the meanwhile he could get together a little more money to build something out of lumber. People said a dugout warmed up real well, held the heat better than a cabin. He just couldn't mind a little dirt sifting down. It would be a good experiment. Dig into the hillside, curl up snug as a coyote or badger. A boar's nest, as people called it. Better than a couple of caves he'd seen here, one of them no more than a rock overhang with a dished-out area littered with scat.

He set aside the shovel and took a few swings with the pick. A pain ran through his ribs, not as sharp as before. He switched to the shovel again and dug out the loose dirt, jabbed some more, and scooped.

When Adam delved and Eve span,
Who was then a gentleman?

Things had changed a little. He was still working with a shovel and sleeping in a tent, but he picked his own tasks now and set his own hours. When he was down in the ditch, he had an image of how the crew might look to a fellow like Nick riding across the plain—a group of hats, inching across the country, flinging dirt up onto a ditch bank. Someone who saw him now might take him for a miner, starting to bore his way into the mountain.

When he estimated he had been at it for two hours, he sidehilled and sat in the shade of a pine tree. With his back to the hillside, he looked out over the plains to the north. He could see forever. Some of the hills in the northeast would be the upper corner of Nebraska, and north of that, some of the Dakota rangeland. In every direction he looked, he saw nothing but vast stretches of land. Not a single building, nor the glint of a windmill blade. He knew there were ranches scattered out there, far and wide, but he couldn't see a sign of them from here.

In back of him, if he climbed the ridge and looked to the south, he would see the town of Willow Springs, some four or five miles away as the land sloped down to the flat plain. He didn't mind having his back to the town, with a pine ridge as barrier, and he rather liked the company of the while clay bluffs, the pines, and the far country. And the two horses. He shifted his gaze to see that they were both in place, picketed and grazing.

In the afternoon he packed his tools and went a mile west to work on salvage. An old stable and shack, at least twenty years old and long fallen into neglect, sat in a sheltered draw. With no one holding title to the property at present, Lane availed himself of the opportunity. With his hammer he knocked apart posts and beams and boards; then with his crowbar he pulled the rusty nails. He put all of the nails in his saddlebag, the best ones to be straightened by lamplight and the worst ones to be stored out of the way of horse and cattle hooves. Some of the posts had rotted at ground level, so he sawed the ends off clean.

Late in the afternoon, a cool breeze came from the northwest and brought gray clouds with it. He put on his jacket and started picking up. He stacked the usable lumber according to length and thickness, judging which pieces would be best for the roof, front wall, door frame, and door of the dugout. At some point he would have to hire a wagon to haul the lumber across to his place, but his main cost consisted of his own labor.

As he was loading up his tools, a horse and rider came over a hill to the west, down into a draw, and up closer. Lane recognized Elbert and one of the Rosette horses, a large sorrel.

Elbert drew rein and sat with both hands on the saddle horn. "Well, how's the hermit?"

"Not too bad. And yourself?"

"Oh, pretty fine. Ol' Nance, though,'bout got fed up with this one kid he put on. Try to teach him somethin', but he cain't get the hang of nothin'."

"Uh-huh. Just the two of you, then, plus Nance?"

"For right now. But Nance is lookin' for someone else. He told me if I knew someone, to let 'im know."

"I'd think about it myself, but I'm just gettin' started here." Lane pointed with his hammer at the lumber.

"'Bout what I thought." A clever look came onto Elbert's face. "Is that where them guys whomped yuh?"

Lane rubbed his fingertip across his cheekbone. "It's just about gone now. Who told you about it?"

"Oh, it got around."

"Huh."

"Ol' Nance, he said he never used his fists. Said that's nigger stuff. If he ever got that mad at a man, he'd put a bullet through 'im. Ah asked if he ever did, and he wouldn't tell me."

"Well, I'm glad I gave you all something to talk about."

"Weren't much. But if you think you ever want to go back and settle up with those two, let me know."

"You and me, cleanin' up the town." Lane gave a short, bitter laugh.

"Suit yourself. Maybe you've had your fill of fighting. But it wouldn't do no harm to get a six-gun. Make them jaspers steer wide of you then." Elbert touched the handle of his own pistol.

"I'll think about it."

Elbert wagged his head and smiled. "Well, you think about the other way, too. Me 'n' my cousin licked two coon hunters from Paducah, come onto our place, and they was a hell of a lot tougher'n these two birds."

"Thanks for the offer, Elbert. I'll stew on it."

"Good enough." Elbert lifted his rein hand. "And if it gits to be too lonesome out here, come on back to the ranch."

"I'll do that. And give my best to Nance."

Lane swabbed the skillet with bacon grease, waited a minute, and laid in two deer steaks. If it gits too lonesome. He poked at the steaks to keep them from sticking. This was just fine, thank you—a whiff of bacon grease, the crackle of meat frying, the austere heat of the campfire.

Get a six-gun. Them jaspers'll steer wide.

He went into the tent for a tin plate, and when he stepped outside, the cool air sharpened the smell of bacon grease in his nostrils. He remembered the sensation. It had happened a couple of times when he spent the month in the line shack. That door had looked out to the north, also.

Things were different now. He had his own equipment, his own place. More confidence in himself, more muscle. He could put this dugout together, get a little sheet-iron stove like the sheepherders used, and brace up for next winter. Maybe find some wage work in the meanwhile. Then see what his next move was.

Lydia had a reserved air about her, wrapped up and holding back. Lane sensed it the moment she opened the door, although she invited him in as always.

"And how are you, Lane?"

"Doing well. And you?"

"Oh, fine. Let me see about getting some coffee." He watched her walk away, but he didn't feel the excitement he had felt before.

When she had the coffee served, she spoke again. "Is everything all right out in the country?"

"Just fine, it seems. I'm putting together a dugout for right now, and then I'll see about a regular cabin."

"It sounds like a perfect adventure."

"I think of it more as an experiment."

"Oh, yes. Self-reliance." Then after a pause, "Have you tried baking a pie yet?"

"No, I haven't. But I think I might. I found some old scraps of fence posts, hard stuff, but too short and twisted for me to use for anything else, and I think they might make good coals for something like that."

"You think things out, don't you?"

"When I can. And yourself?"

"Oh, yes, but not to the degree of planning which firewood I'll use next." Then with a light laugh she said, "I suppose I do think of some things in advance, such as what to wear next Sunday."

"My uppermost thought," he said, laughing with her.

"So I take it you're pleased with the place you settled on."

"Yes, I am. Now that I'm there, I realize that being on the north side might be colder and a little more difficult in the winter than if I had found a parcel facing south, but I'm satisfied with what I have."

"That's good. And it sounds as if you keep things simple."

"I try."

"It must be nice to be away from town."

"Well, town has its pleasant features," he said, trying a gallant smile, "but I don't mind having it behind me most of the time."

"Such a little town, and yet it has its complications, doesn't it?"

"It seems to."

"Didn't you find it that way, when you lived here?" She had her arms folded across her front, and she gave him a look that seemed to have more than small talk behind it.

He took a deep breath. "Well, yes, I did. I suppose you've heard something about it, so I don't think I need to give a detailed account."

"I wouldn't want you to feel that you had to."

"Thank you. And even if my version might be different in some ways, I expect the general outline would not change."

She nodded.

"I also recognize that if two people are going to—let us say—decide whether they are going to continue seeing each other—they like to have some understanding of one another's past."

"It's considerate of you to recognize that. Every person by this stage in life has a past of some kind, and I try to respect the other person's privacy. But at the same time, as you say, one needs a minimal understanding."

He took another breath. "With respect, then, to this one aspect of my past, which seems to be in the realm of common knowledge, I can say that I try to think of it as something I've been through and am trying to put behind me."

"That is very well expressed. But I notice that you speak in the present. Still trying."

He weighed the comment, shifting his head to each side. "I suppose so. I thought I had it packed away, but as you may have heard, a little trouble came up the last time I left here."

"I didn't know it happened just then, but I heard that some of the old trouble came to the surface again."

"Well, to be a little more direct, again without going into details, a couple of fellows here in town decided they wanted to get their licks in on me, and some of this old trouble, as you call it, figured in as a main motive. But these two chaps seem to dislike anything I do, and they dog me when I'm doing something so simple as visiting here." From her stiffened expression he realized he might have said more than he needed to. "It seems as if all this might be distasteful to you."

"Let me try to make a distinction, if I may. This thing that transpired before, I see as an episode in itself that you are trying to put in your past. Whether I find that distasteful perhaps does not matter, or I could say perhaps it is not my right to judge it. But if the trouble is not over, and it still comes around, and it takes the shape of men following you from my door and accosting you on the street—"

"I have to agree with you. And even if there happens to be some perverse jealousy in operation, on the part of one if not both of these fellows, things would not have taken this shape, as you call it, if I hadn't done something to begin with."

"That's an admirable statement of responsibility."

She had a cordial tone, but he could tell a distance had fallen between them. Her physical presence, which once had seemed compatible with his, now seemed withdrawn beyond his reach.

"Thank you. But to put it in a nutshell, I can see that I am a person whose life is not as free of complications as you would be comfortable with."

Her face took on a sympathetic expression. "I wouldn't say that that summarizes you fairly, but I do not disagree, and I think you said it rather well."

"In other words, my understanding is matched only by my skill at speech."

She laughed. "We get along far too well not to be friends. Please do not think I'm harsh on you."

"I don't. I can see it clearly enough. And I appreciate your willingness to be a friend."

"Please count me as one. And I hope you aren't troubled too much more by these . . . ruffians."

"I don't think I will be. If I was as good with my fists as I am with words, they wouldn't have given me as much trouble as they did."

"Spoken like a man."

As she laughed, he could tell she was laughing with him at his troubles, as a friend should.

Lane dropped the rock onto the loose dirt next to his excavation, then squared his shoulders back and took a long, deep breath. He counted his collection, as he did each time he lugged a rock up the hill. A dozen. The farther he had to carry them and the more he had to climb, the heavier they got. This last one had to weigh over a hundred pounds, and it brought sweat to his legs as well as to his arms and chest.

He climbed to the top of the ridge, where he could often find a mild breeze. As soon as his face cleared the top, he caught the cool air. Climbing a few more feet until he found a level spot, he took off his hat and looked around to the north again.

The two horses were grazing, unbothered. Too bad he couldn't rig up some way of getting them to move the rocks. Other men probably had devised ways, such as a sling or a drag, but he didn't have any materials and didn't know much about improvising his own harness.

He wondered how big a stone he could carry. Once when he was a boy, he saw a strong man at the circus who picked up and carried a rock of about four hundred pounds. The man came from Spain, and according to the impresario, he developed his skill by clearing rocks from the fields in his native country. A giant brute of a man, he had an alien look on his face, as if to say he would have little to share with these onlookers even if he spoke their language.

Lane turned and let the breeze ripple across his damp forehead. He looked up at the blue sky, bright with cottony clouds, then around at the pale bluffs rising out of the ridge higher up. Two buzzards were soaring in the air currents high above the ramparts.

He lowered his gaze and rubbed his neck muscles. Down the slope, the dozen rocks sat waiting to be added to. Once he started the walls, the rocks would get used up fast. He wondered how much he would have to feed the foreign giant if he could get him to comb the hills for a pile of rocks. Huh. Better off alone. He would need a lot of small and medium-sized ones as well, and he had time.

Nick's lessons came back to him from time to time, especially whenever he had to work with the horses. With the use of a barrel hitch on his riding saddle, he hauled the short, crooked fence posts back to his camp. They splintered too much when he tried cutting them with his ax, so he took out his small buck saw and cut them into firewood lengths.

Rather than start the fire and let it burn down as he mixed the ingredients, he thought it better to make the pie first. He didn't want to waste good firewood if the whole thing turned into a mess. First he set the dried apples soaking in a pan. Then in his dishpan he mixed the dry ingredients, poured in some bacon grease softened in the sun, and worked up a ball of dough. With an empty bottle donated by Tom Sedley, he rolled out the crust on the floured top of his little makeshift table. He laid the bottom crust into the pie tin, drained the water off the apples and mixed in the sugar and cinnamon, and scraped the filling into the shell. Then he laid on the top crust, trimmed and pinched it all the way around, and cut a few holes for ventilation. Lydia was right. It didn't have a great deal of mystery to it, and besides, he had watched a few ranch cooks and knew what the process was supposed to look like.

He covered the pie in the Dutch oven and built the fire. As the firewood was burning down to coals, he hauled medium-sized rocks for his pile, making quick trips to check on the fire each time. When he had a good bed of coals, he set the three-legged Dutch oven in the center.

An hour and a quarter later, the top crust was dry and turning dark brown. With his pot hook he lifted the oven from the coals and set it on the ground. Then he took out the pie and left it on the table to cool.

That evening, when he had built the fire back up and had cooked some deer meat, he cut open the pie for dessert. The filling had shrunk, and the apple slices took a bit of chewing. Lydia had said he could use either dried or fresh apples, but he imagined she had given him a recipe assuming fresh ones. Next time, he would cook some moisture into the apples.

Nevertheless, it was edible, and not bad for his

first try. He made it alone, and he would eat it alone, here in the company of his horses, his pile of stones, the pine trees with here and there a cedar, and buzzards soaring above the dun-colored bluffs. He could eat a second piece later, after dark, he could have some for breakfast, and he would still have some for noon dinner. Much better than having to give it to the giant.

The sun went down behind the bluffs to the west. It was moving north each day, and before long it would be setting beyond the buttes, way out on the plain. This side of the ridge would get hotter in the daytime then, too. But for the time being, dusk fell early and the air cooled.

He stirred the embers and held out his palms to take in the warmth. This whole experiment was interesting, but he wondered if he was just marking his time, waiting for something. He had time to do things the hard way, the slow way, and when he cut a notch in the stick he did not worry about how much he had accomplished that day. Today, for example—he had spent the whole day fetching wood and baking a pie, and he felt satisfied. Self-reliant, as Lydia said. Alone but not despondent. Waiting for something. He wondered if he was waiting for the train in a country where the tracks did not run.

He wasn't waiting for a woman to show up. Although he had the passing fancy, he never expected Cora or any other woman to come to him. The same held true now. No one but Elbert was going to come to his encampment on the breaks. It served him well as a refuge, but he was going to have to take the initiative, go up and over and back out into the world to find what was not going to come to him.

What was it? Not a train or a coach, or a giant come to help him gather rocks, or a woman floating over the mountain with a golden pie in her hands. It was something he had to find. Not a nugget on the mountainside, a treasure chest in an old Indian cave, a jewel in the belly of a beast. Nothing he could see or touch. It was an answer, the answer to a question left in the air since the curtain came down.

He, the one praised for his way with words, could phrase it in various ways. If things had ended, why were they not over? What did their love mean? Was he something to lie about, or was their love the real thing? He had pondered the big question, not often in words, every day since he had seen her last. When he reduced it to the two options, was it A or was it B? he could not accept either as the whole answer. And so he deferred it, thinking perhaps that the answer would become clearer with the passage of time.

It hadn't. The only thing he was sure of was that time had passed, he had acquired some streaks of gray, and he still had the uncertainty in him. He also had it in him to do something—not wait out here until he had a Rip Van Winkle beard growing to his waist. He had waited long enough. Tomorrow he could wash some clothes, finish up the pie, and start looking for an answer.

He felt the excitement of getting ready for a trip. With his camp set in order, he took both horses into town and left them in the stable. It was not yet midday, and he thought he could catch Emma at a time when Douglas was still at the store. In the past when he thought about going to Emma's house, though he never did, he had to worry about crossing paths with Joseph. That danger had passed, though, as Joseph had taken Frances, the plump little schoolteacher, and set her up as wife and missus in the house that Collier built. The last time Lane had seen Joseph and Frances, she looked as if she was hiding a loaf under an apron.

When Emma answered the door, the first thing he noticed was gray in her hair. The second was Trixie, wide-eyed in long blond curls, standing behind her mother and holding a rag doll.

"Well, hello, Lane. I didn't expect to see you." Emma's hand went to her hair, then settled to her side. "Would you like to come in for a minute?"

"Thank you." He took off his hat and stepped into the living room, which looked the same as before except that a pile of clean laundry sat on the sofa. He glanced through the kitchen door and saw the blue willowware in the cabinet.

Emma stood back in the middle of the living room with her hands clasped in front of her. "And what can I do for you today, Lane? I hope everything is well with you."

"Yes, things are all right." He gave a nod that he hoped conveyed assurance. "I've come to ask a favor."

A trace of worry appeared around her eyes. "What kind of a favor?"

"I would like to ask you if you know where Cora is." He felt the strangeness and the boldness of saying her name out loud in this town.

She hesitated with a slow intake of breath. "I don't know how wise it would be. Everything that happened here went very rough on her, as I'm sure you know."

"Well, they did on me, too, and I'm sure you know that. I also know that it caused you some discomfort, for which I offer my apologies." He felt buoyed by the formality that came to him. "So it is with some deliberation that I come to ask your help."

"What do you intend to do?"

"I don't have a firm plan, but what I hope to do is resolve some questions that got left hanging."

"I thought everything ended."

"Things came to an end, but I was never satisfied in knowing whether it was what she wanted. Maybe I should say, even though things seemed to end, they didn't for me, and I would like to know whether they did for her. That's what I need to find out. If they did, I get an answer, and if they didn't, I guess I get an understanding."

"I can't tell you that. Cora and I were friends, but

deep down, it always seemed she couldn't say what she really felt."

"I think you're right, and I wouldn't expect you to give me a definitive answer. But if I could talk to her, or if she flatly told me she didn't wish to speak with me, I could arrive at some resolution."

"My advice would be to leave things alone, but from your perseverance I can infer that you've tried doing that."

"That's very accurate. And all I'm asking is whether you know where she is. I'm not asking for an address, just the town."

Emma took another slow breath. "The last I heard, which was a little over a year ago, she was still living in Laramie City."

"With her husband and children, I suppose."

"Yes, that's where they went when they left here."

"Thank you, Emma. I won't forget your kind help."

"You're welcome, and I hope no harm comes of it."

"I'll do my best. And thanks again."

The cold wind was blowing in Laramie when he stepped off the train. As he walked downtown, he saw that the lilac bushes were putting on their tight little purple buds the size of bird shot. They had already bloomed and wilted in Emma's front yard and elsewhere in Willow Springs, so he estimated that the higher elevation made a difference of two or three weeks. The shade trees had not leafed out yet either, and the windblown dust gave the town a desolate atmosphere. But he could imagine Cora's presence here, and after the long train ride to Cheyenne and the shorter one to Laramie, he was going to stretch his legs and see something of the place.

In the downtown area, he took a room in a place called the Crown Hotel. With his bags put away, he went out again. He walked to the edge of town and past the penitentiary, with its stone walls and barred windows. From there he walked about a mile to the university, with its granite buildings and struggling lawns. He paused at the edge of the campus and appreciated the presence of learning. In these buildings, here on the high, cold plain, scholars kept up the pursuit of traditional ideas in areas such as natural science, law, and literature, and they also found a place for new studies, such as the dinosaur findings not far to the west of here. The place gave a feeling of reassurance.

Downtown again, he found a café where he could eat his evening meal and let his feelings settle in. This was the town where Cora had come to live. She had probably sat in this café; she had no doubt walked down many of the same streets he had just walked. She might or might not still live here.

After his meal, he went out onto the street and found a hack driver who looked discreet and trustworthy. The man said he had not heard of that last name but could probably find out about it through his fellow drivers.

Twenty minutes later, the man came back with

an address on Garfield Street. He said the house was dark at the present.

Lane handed him an envelope. "This is a note for the lady at that address. It is important that it not fall into anyone else's hands, so if it doesn't get delivered until tomorrow, that's fine. In fact, it might be more convenient. If she chooses to write back, you can leave the message here with me at the Crown Hotel. The letter says I'm in town, but it doesn't say where. You're free to tell her, but to anyone else, I'm just someone on the street." Lane held out a silver dollar. "Is this adequate to the task?"

The driver closed one droopy eye. "Quite so."

As the horse clattered away, Lane went into another café and asked if he could drink a glass of beer by the window. The waiter said yes and showed him to a table.

He pictured the hack driver wheeling away in the evening, the envelope tucked in a coat pocket. Lane was filled with a sense that he had taken a big step, one that could not be retrieved. It might be an ill-advised move, one that would qualify him for the fool of fools, but he had done something.

Chapter Eleven

As Lane sat drinking coffee by the café window the next morning, he saw her. Beautiful Cora. She walked out of a pharmacy, hailed a cab, and was gone. It hit him like a jolt, and he took a minute or two to absorb the impact and to assure himself he had done well not to jump up and run out after her. He reasoned through it. He didn't want to approach her unexpected on the street. If she had not responded to his note, all the more reason not to complicate things; if she had, he would hear from her soon enough.

He was sitting in his room reading *Madame Bovary*, which he had read several years earlier, when a knock came at the door. When he answered, a hotel clerk told him a lady had come by and said she could meet with Mr. Weller at one that afternoon in the lobby downstairs. Lane thanked the clerk and went back to his chair.

With a look at his watch, he saw he had two and

a half hours to wait. He was glad he had a book. He picked it up, but after reading a couple of pages and realizing he hadn't followed it at all, he set it aside. Was she afraid to write a note? Was she out running errands and left the message in person to save time? Had she hoped to bump into him in the lobby? He told himself it didn't matter, and he made himself return to the study of French provincial life.

At a little after noon he ate in the café where he had eaten that morning as well as the night before. As he watched the street, tensing at every hack and carriage that came along, he tried to subdue his excitement. She wouldn't arrive until one or later, and there was no use looking out for her.

Shortly before one he took a chair in the lobby, a wooden armchair with padded armrests and seat. The desk clerk who had delivered the message glanced up under a lowered brow and resumed sorting papers. Lane settled in and tried to be patient, watching the door and windows and occasionally checking the clock behind the desk.

Then she was coming through the door, Cora in a gray dress and coat, walking at a pace that seemed at once hurried and reluctant.

He rose, walked forward to meet her, and took her hands in his.

"I'm here," she said. Her blue-gray eyes, uncertain, roved as they met his. "I didn't recognize you at first with the beard."

"It's the gray."

She stood half a step away, with her hands still touching his. "You look good. You look—distinguished."

"Thank you. You look fine, too."

"I don't think I do. I think I look haggard, worn out. Old." She looked down at her dress.

"Oh, come on. I saw you on the street earlier in the day, and I thought you were the best-looking woman in town."

"Far from it." She lowered her hands, and he let his fall away.

"Thank you for coming. I found out from Emma that you lived here, but I didn't know if you wanted to see me."

"I didn't either. Well, I did, but I was afraid."

"Afraid of what someone might do to you?"

"Not so much that. More afraid of what might happen. That everything might start all over again." Her eyes roved across his.

"Well, nothing has to happen if you don't want it to." He looked around. The desk clerk was making busy. "Shall we sit down?"

They found two chairs back from the window.

"And how have you been, Cora?"

Her eyes still moved a little. "Oh, all right. It's a life. And you?"

"Oh, I'm fine. Getting along." He saw now that she had a few gray hairs herself, as well as a general cloudiness in her face.

"Do you still live there?"

"In Willow Springs? Not exactly. I was on a ranch for a while. A couple of years. Then I settled on a piece of land of my own. Not much, but I like it so far."

Her eyes were moist. "You've been all alone."

"I tried to meet someone else, but it didn't work well. But that's not why I wanted to look you up."

Her eyes steadied. "Was there some other reason?"

"I didn't think things were over. And I can tell now they weren't."

"Oh, Lane, they'll never be over. I've loved you all this time, but there was nothing to be done."

"Day after day, then year after year, I thought, things just didn't end. You never really terminated them."

"I couldn't." Her voice had a faint sob. "I didn't end things decisively because I couldn't end things forever with you. I'm sorry. I suppose it was selfish of me. I couldn't give you up."

"Well, I didn't want to be given up."

"And so you've just been—working? Have you gone places, done things? How have you spent this time?"

He wanted to tell her everything at once—how much she meant to him, how many times he had walked past her empty house, how he had seen her in the landscape. He made himself focus on details. "I went to work on a ranch. Actually, I worked for a while with a ditch-cleaning crew, and then I went to the ranch. I worked there two seasons, and I spent most of each winter there as well. I learned to get by, do things with my hands."

"And trips? Have you gone anywhere?"

"One winter I went to Nebraska. I wanted to see Cedar Canyon, where you grew up, so when I had some time, I did it."

Her face showed surprise. "You did! I haven't been back in a long time. I wish I could go there."

"I know the way."

She gave a pained smile. "I would really like that."

"I know. But you can't." He hesitated for a few seconds, then went on. "So how are you getting along with McGee?"

She shrugged and looked down. "Oh, all right. Like I said, it's a life. I'm doing what I'm supposed to do."

"And he's prospering, I imagine? On his way to his first million?"

"So he hopes."

"I was surprised you were able to get away from the house today."

"He's not at home right now. I had a lot of errands, so I made it seem as if I had one more to do this afternoon. Actually, I did. Here." She glanced at the clock. "But I didn't plan on being gone for long."

"I didn't know what to expect—how long we would meet, or how it would be."

"Like I said, I was afraid."

"I suppose I could say I was apprehensive—mostly worried that you wouldn't want to see me or that you wouldn't be able."

She smiled. "Well, you see? That worry is gone."

"It sure is. And after this? What do you think? I can stay in town a few days, if you think we would meet again."

"I would like that."

"I don't want to get you into trouble again."

"You won't."

"It wasn't supposed to happen before."

"I know. I think I have more strength now, more resistance."

"I'm glad to hear that. And we don't have to do anything extreme. I'm content with meeting like this. It's safe."

"Yes, it is."

"What do you think of tomorrow or the next day, then?"

"I can let you know. I can either send a message or drop by like I did earlier."

"If you do that, don't be afraid to send for me. I'll come bounding down the stairs."

"Oh, you dear boy. I know you would."

They stood up together, he took her hands again, and they brushed their lips in a kiss. As he watched her walk away, she stopped at the door, turned, and waved. He smiled and winked as he waved back, and she walked out the door. Beautiful Cora.

He sat down and took a couple of deep breaths. What a charged atmosphere there had been in this little space. Almost afraid to get too close, each of them keeping a distance, but a clear confirmation that everything he thought was true.

* * *

That night he yielded to the temptation he had resisted the night before. He walked past her house on Garfield Street. Lamplight shone in the front room, where the shade was drawn. A shadow moved but did not fall directly on the shade.

He thought once more of the few minutes they had spent together in the hotel lobby, and he could not believe how much he valued that short space of time.

The next day at a little after ten, the clerk appeared with the news that a lady was waiting in the lobby below. Lane thanked him and handed him a twenty-five-cent piece.

Cora was sitting in the same chair as the day before. She was wearing a sky-blue dress with buttons of the same color. As Lane took her hand, he saw that her eyes were steadier today.

"So glad you could make it. No trouble, I hope." He sat down.

"Someone is in Cheyenne."

"Making connections with people of power and influence?"

"I think he thinks so."

"Just as well. I'm glad I didn't come a few days later, and meet him on the train." He scanned her face and saw discomfort there. "And how was your evening?"

"All right, I guess. I couldn't sleep at all."

"Neither could I. Too much to go through, over and over. I didn't mind it, though."

"Actually, I didn't either. It meant so much to me that you would come to see me. But it left me in something of a state of turmoil." She looked over at the clock. "I don't have much time today," she said, "but I might have a little more tomorrow."

"That's all right. I can stay that long. I don't know how much we can jump into a topic with just a few minutes, but I appreciate your dropping by." He reached across and took her hand.

"I'm glad to be able to. I don't have a clear outlook on where things might go, but after seeing you yesterday, I knew for sure that things had never ended and that I wanted to see you again."

"I don't know how far we should go, either. For now, I'm satisfied in knowing that we've felt the same, neither of us ceasing to love the other or think about the other."

"I never did. I wondered if you did, if you found someone to try to help you—but you didn't."

He paused to frame his words. "We both gave up a great deal. You gave up your freedom, and your hope to ever be treated well, and I gave up the hope that we could be together."

She nodded.

"And I spent many long hours thinking about how things went wrong, and the things I did wrong. I'll state it in words. I lifted my hand against another man's family. But I never thought I deserved to take you away or to win you in battle. I thought that if things were so bad that you could leave him, we could be together. But things didn't happen that way, of course, and as time passed I came to believe that the one thing I deserved was an answer to my question of whether things really ended."

"Which they didn't."

"So here I am now, not exactly where we were before, wondering if something might happen after all."

"We're not dead yet."

"I was afraid *you* were—spiritually, I mean. It seemed to me that I went to sleep, in some ways, for a long while. Now things are waking up."

Her eyes were moist. "I've always felt that you knew me better than anyone else ever has. I *was* dead, or I felt that way. And now I feel alive again with you."

"Do you remember a time, in one of our early conversations, when I told you I was looking for something to believe in?"

"Of course I do. I've always remembered that."

"Well, I'm still looking for it. That's what brought me here. Even if I had gotten a different answer, I would have been working on that quest."

"Oh, and I love you for it."

"And I love you, Cora. Nothing has stopped that." He went soft inside as their eyes met, and then he braced himself up. "What I'm wondering now is whether, on the basis of having taken our punishment and put in our time, we deserve a chance at seeing if things could go our way after all. To put it in unabashed terms, I wonder if true love might prevail."

"It sounds so noble the way you say it."

"I know. But I wonder if it is realistic."

"That we could be happy?"

"No, I don't doubt that. I wonder if you could summon up the resistance. You said something yesterday to the effect that you were gaining strength."

A cloudiness came into her features. "He's done some things that might make it easier to do something."

"And as you observed so acutely, we're not dead yet."

"No, we sure aren't."

He leaned to kiss her, and before he closed his eyes he saw that hers, against the background of her dress, were as blue as willowware.

In the early afternoon of the following day, as Lane was working his way into a slower novel of life in provincial France and thinking he should have reread it as the first of the two, the desk clerk knocked on his door. He had the same message as the day before, and Lane gave him the same compensation. After letting the clerk get a good head start, he went downstairs to meet Cora.

She was wearing an outfit he remembered well, a red blouse with black buttons, and a full-length black skirt. Her dark hair fell loose to her shoulders. She rose to give him her hand as he approached her, and he saw that the skirt and blouse still set off her figure to advantage. He kissed her in greeting, and they sat down.

"And how is everything today?" he asked.

She gave a sigh expressing relief. "I still have a little freedom. Not much time, but what's mine is mine for right now."

"That's good." He took her hand and rubbed it. "Are you keeping yourself from getting too nervous about all this?"

"Yes. And thank you for caring."

"I don't want you to regret seeing me again. Not in any way."

"I don't."

"You look so good."

"I wish I felt that way."

"You look restored."

"Well, he's left me alone somewhat for the last little while. I don't mean he's let me live alone, but that he hasn't been so overwhelming, leaning over my shoulder on everything."

"An exercise in Christian forbearance?"

Her eyes went up to her brows. "I doubt it. He was in financial difficulties for a while, but he improved his circumstances."

"Oh, did he land a big fish?"

"Something like that." She lowered her gaze and moved her hands. "Let's not talk about him. What were we on before that?"

"I was telling you how good you look."

"Oh, yes. And how much I didn't think I deserved it."

"Honestly, you do. You've kept your vitality."

"Well, I've kept active, but I'm not working myself into the ground as much as before. In his recent flush of prosperity, he's let me have a washwoman." She shook her head. "Oh, there I am, talking about him again."

"We were talking about you. Let me go on. You've kept your figure, and your hair still looks beautiful." He brushed it with the back of his fingers. "Some women let their figure go, and when they do, they quit taking interest in their hair. They chop it off, or tie it up and hardly ever wash it. At least, those are things that I've noticed." He took her hand again and rubbed her fingernails with the tips of his first two fingers. "See? When these little half-moons look healthy, as they do now, that means things are in good balance."

She smiled. "You always make me feel so much like a woman."

He made a motion with his eyebrows. "It's all there. You just need someone to bring it out. Like the strings of an instrument."

"You haven't changed a bit. You're still pretty good yourself."

"With words?"

"Not just that. At bringing out the music."

He let the wave subside for a few seconds. "And so you have a little time to yourself this afternoon."

"Not much."

"An hour?"

"Maybe that."

"Is there somewhere you'd like to go—for a walk? Have some coffee?"

She shrugged. "No. Right here is all right."

His eyes met hers. "Is there any place else you'd like to go?"

"I don't know." She looked down.

"Against your better judgment?"

"I don't know how much judgment rules in all of this."

"More a matter of fear, or apprehension?"

"Yes, more that. I'm afraid that if we do anything, we'll start everything all over again."

"And you don't want that?"

She lifted her eyes, and they were steady gray. "I want some of it. I want what we had before." Now she took his hand. "Oh, Lane, you don't know how much I want you. Why else would I come and see you three days in a row?"

"But you're afraid. And I don't blame you. You don't want the consequences."

"That."

"What if the consequences were, or included, your being free?"

She sighed. "That's the difference between us. You always know what you want."

"I suppose I do. I want you. Of course. But I also want that something bigger—I want to believe in love. I want to believe in something bigger than you or me, either one, but I also want to believe in you, that you have the self-determination—"

"But you want just me, too, don't you?"

"Yes, of course. I just said that."

"Would you make another trip here, even if we didn't do everything we wanted on this trip?"

He reflected. "Well, yes. Sure I would." He tipped his head. "After a respectable amount of time? Or to give you time to make up your mind for sure?"

Her eyes were full of desire. "I've already made up my mind."

"Well, then, let's say that I've been to the range and back."

"When did you get into town?"

"Just a few minutes ago. But fortunately, I'm not fatigued from my trip."

In his room, he tried to do everything at once—caress her, kiss her all over, undress her. With a great effort of self-discipline, he made himself break it down into small sequences. Undress her a little, caress her, kiss her. Roll her over slowly, lift her ankle to his shoulder, kiss the indentation between heel and calf, caress her calf, kiss the underside of her knee. When he had them both fully undressed, restraint broke away, time vanished, and he was merged with her as always.

It was magic, unbelievable. Everything that had been taken away from him—her breasts, her buttocks, her thighs, her midsection—everything he had remembered with such incredulity when he was alone, in exile as it now seemed—he had free access to it all again. Like a dream. Adrift in the river of time. There had been no time. There had been time, and the treasure had come to him again.

He lay on top of her, their motion having come to its climax. Supporting himself on his elbows, he ran the fingers of both hands through her dark, beautiful hair. He kissed her on the lips, all over her face.

"Cora. Beautiful Cora. The girl I loved and was afraid I might not ever see again."

"Oh, Lane. I love you. I have always loved you. As if we were in love before we ever met."

"I thought of you a hundred times, a thousand times a day. And I could never mention your name, not to anyone. When I said it out loud, by myself, not very often, it sounded strange and faraway."

"Say my name now," she said, pressing his buttocks.

"Cora. Beautiful Cora. My lovely Cora. Mine again, Cora."

"Yes, Lane. Yours again."

They lay apart, warm from the exertion and perspiring in spite of the coolness of the room.

"It's still like a dream," he said. "As if the seven lean years, the drought and the famine, have passed. The long period of waiting, like Jacob, who loved Rachel so much and put in so many years to have her."

"You made me yours again."

"Leah and Rachel, all in one, and the same girl as always. Oh, I love you, Cora." He kissed both her breasts. "It seemed like so long, and the waiting was so open-ended. I was afraid to hope. At least Jacob had an agreement, or a contract."

"You know I can't give you any guarantee, but I'm going to try to get away."

"I know." He kissed her on the abdomen, just below her navel.

"Do you remember what you told me the last time we were together like this?"

"Oh, I imagine I said a good many things. Which one do you have in mind?"

"You said the next time you had me in your arms, you were going to put a bun in my oven."

He laughed. "I said that? I don't remember it."

"Yes, you did."

"Huh. I must not have let myself remember. There's not much danger of that right now, is there?"

"I don't think so. I've kept pretty good track of the days."

"I knew you always did, so I assumed things were all right today."

"They are."

He patted her leg. "Well, it was brave talk then. I would suppose we're both past the point where it would be feasible to have a bouncy little Trixie."

"Oh, my. I bet she's getting bigger, too."

"Up on her own feet, that's for sure."

Her hand touched his. "But, yes, I think you're right. My own children are big enough now that I wouldn't want to go through that part again. But I don't like to tell you that you have to give up that dream, if you don't want to."

"It's all right. I've thought about it, and I've gotten used to the idea of not having children of my own. And in a way, it makes me feel as if it has helped me earn something."

"Really?"

"Yes, it's as if giving up that part adds something to the credit side of the ledger. For both of us. If we've given up that time together when we might have had children, then that's part of our larger concession."

"I see."

"The way I've explained it to myself is, we gave each other up for a larger reason. Not just buckling to authority, though there was some of that, but also leaving you free, if I could say it that way, to tend to your own family. At the risk of telling you what your own motives were, I can say that I've granted the primacy of family as the main reason we both acquiesced."

"I'm willing to go along with that."

"And continuing with that line of thought, if we've given up and given in, we may have earned at least the right to try again now."

"My children are a little older now, but I am still a ways away from fulfilling my responsibilities with them."

"To borrow a phrase, I'm willing to go along with that."

She smiled.

"There's one claim I'm not so willing to grant, though."

"Which one is that?"

"The claim of possession that this fellow seems to think he has over you, as if you were his property."

"He's always been like that."

"I just don't accept it. I may be too modern for

my own good, but I don't think anyone has the right to do what he did that day in the empty house. By my way of thinking, he renounced some of this rights when he did that."

"He thought he strengthened them. There was a time, earlier, when he used to shave his initial in my hair down there."

"Like a brand?"

"Yes. At first he did it like it was all in fun, and then it became more possessive, so I asked him not to do it anymore. This was in the first few years we were married."

"Uh-huh."

"Then that day, when he did the thing to me, he told me, when he was finished, that he wondered if he should shave in his initial again, or even shave a question mark. Really contemptuous, but he didn't do anything like that."

"It looks much better the way it is. All complete. And it doesn't belong to anyone else but you."

"I'm glad you think so."

"Sweet little chamber of Venus." He planted a kiss on the outside.

"Oh, I love you so much," she said, pulling him to her.

"And I love you, Cora. After all the time I spent alone, in what I thought of as my lone winter, when I was afraid to hope, and now to be together like this again."

"You can hope now," she said. "That season is over. I'm not going to lose you this time."

* * *

On the return trip, engrossing himself in the exploits of Julien Sorel and Madame de Rênal, he paid little attention to the other passengers. The train made a slow climb out of Laramie and a long descent into Cheyenne. After a layover of three and a half hours, he took the train north through Chugwater and Wheatland. During that part of the trip, it became too dark to read. He was glad to get off in Orin, where he carried his bags to the livery stable and paid for the keep of his two horses. With the bags tied onto the sorrel, he swung into the saddle on the bay.

He put up for the night in Shawnee, got an early start the next morning, and rode through Willow Springs at about noon. The large double doors of the blacksmith shop were open, and a hammering of metal on metal sounded from within. The blows continued as Newt Collier, wearing a hickory shirt and no apron, came to the door and stood watching. When the clanging stopped, Collier turned and called something to the person inside. The noise resumed, and Collier lifted his chin and watched Lane ride by.

That was fine. He could practice his insolent gaze all he wanted, and share his dry husks of intelligence with his fellow spy, who probably had his hands in his apron and was peeping out the window of Apley's store at that moment.

CHAPTER TWELVE

Lane handed Cora a small bundle wrapped in tissue paper. She set it in her lap and pushed herself up to sit straighter against the bedstead. After draping the sheet across her front, she hefted the bundle.

"It's heavy."

"Then it's not a pair of socks."

"Or a girdle." She lifted the paper with one hand as the bundle shifted in the other. "It's in two pieces." She pulled back the wrapping all the way around and revealed the ornate pair of spurs, black with inlaid gold roses along the sides and tipped with silver rowels. "Oh, Lane," she said. "They're beautiful."

"I thought a ranch girl might appreciate something like this." He settled into bed next to her and kissed her. "They're for the two of us. One for you and one for me, and then when we're together as a couple, the pair will be complete."

"How romantic. Like tokens in a romance. Golden chalices."

"Pick one for yourself."

"Let's see. The roses go on the outside, so this is the left one. I'll take it." She set up both spurs in her lap as if they were characters in a puppet theater. With a soft, high voice she said, "Will you miss me when I'm gone?" She moved the other spur and spoke for it. "Day and night, my darling." Then she put down both spurs and opened her arms to Lane. "Come to me, my gallant knight."

A little later, she said she had to get dressed and be going. "This has been very nice," she said as she pulled on her dress. "Four walls. Our little world, all to ourselves."

"Will you be able to take your token with you?"

"Of course."

"I wouldn't want it to fall into evil hands."

"It won't." She presented her front to him so he could button her blouse as he sat on the bed. "By the way, I've arranged a means for you to write to me or leave messages if you need to."

"Oh, really?"

"Yes. The washwoman I mentioned. Mrs. Rutherford. She lives on Fourth Street, a few blocks from me. I'll write her address down so you'll have it."

"That sounds handy. I don't know that I'll be writing long, florid letters. I still feel plundered from before. But for practical purposes of communication, it's a good idea. I take it she's rather discreet?"

"Oh, yes."

"She's met him?"

"Yes, with all his condescending manner."

"Oh. Uh-huh. I believe you mentioned before that it was something of a measure of his recent rise in prosperity."

"So it seems. He likes to be able to pay a workingwoman to help out. He lets her know how bountiful he is, and he tells me I get 'treated like a queen.' Those are his words."

"He seems to get some benefit from his status, then."

"All he can. And it makes me shudder."

"Well, if he's spending his own money, it's not quite as brazen as before."

She tensed, and the button slipped from his fingertips.

"Oh. Sorry. I didn't mean to touch on an old sore spot."

"It just makes me sick. I mean sick through and through."

"That old business?"

"No. The way he got this new money."

"Oh, has he been up to something?"

"Yes, and I can't abide it."

"Is it something you can talk about?"

"Yes and no. I've been repulsed by it. I've wanted to tell someone about it, tell you about it, but it's just so ugly."

"Uh-huh."

"He's a thief."

Lane waited a second, to respect her tone of finality, and then he said, "Well, that's not anything new. From what you told me before, and from what I've heard on my own, he has a habit of making free with other people's merchandise and assets."

"This more recent business is more outright theft than anything I knew of from before. And it entails larger amounts of money."

Lane took heart at the sound of it. "Did he abscond with someone else's funds?"

"Not quite that simple, and I don't know all the details. And, oh! He can't find out I've told anybody."

"He's sure not going to get it from me." He pulled her to him and kissed her bosom. "Tell me what you want, and don't worry."

She let out a heavy sigh and sat on the edge of the bed with him. "He says it's all covered up and nobody can find out, but he is very insistent, in a menacing way, that no one know about it."

"Then that's exactly the type of thing that ought to get out. But that's up to you. Go ahead."

She took a breath and exhaled it. "He got into a scheme with a friend of his, someone he knew in Nebraska and maybe before that. We'll leave him nameless, just call him X. One of the reasons, probably the main one, that we came to Laramie was that X had moved here."

"And what line of work is he in?"

"Insurance and assessments. He represents insurance companies and does assessments on his own."

"So I imagine your husband does some work for him."

"Yes. Some of it, I'm sure, is aboveboard, but

some of it seems to be shady. As in the case in Nebraska, they find land claims that are abandoned, and someone goes out and acquires signatures."

"Someone being McGee?"

"I think he may have done some of the signing, and in other cases he's found people to sign, but which people I don't know."

"That's probably not a quick way to a million."

"No, it isn't. The property is usually in small parcels, not of very high value, and some of it doesn't sell very fast if at all. And someone hasn't been very satisfied with its not being, as you say, a quick way."

"I see. So he had to move into something better?"

"Yes. It's all my fault, of course, according to him. It's cost him so much to keep his wife."

"Whereas another person might interpret that he feels he needs money to cut a good figure in life, and he can't make it by the usual means."

"Exactly. We've been together nearly fifteen years, and he was at it before that, and he keeps ending up in the same place, in terms of how much he has."

"So he decided not to enter by the strait gate."

"Yes. He got impatient, and he and X put their heads together, and they came up with a scheme to defraud an insurance company."

"Loss of property? Loss of life?"

"Loss of life. I don't know exactly how it worked, but they didn't cause anyone's death. They took out a policy on a person who was dying, and they set it up to look as if he was in good health. I think someone posed for this identity. And then when the real person died, they collected the death benefit. I think someone also posed as the son, for purposes of collecting the check and signing it."

"He's a regular fraud and forger, isn't he?"

"I'm just sick about it. And he tells me he did it for his family. As if the children and I made demands on him."

"So he made a good haul?"

Her eyes widened. "I should say so. Thousands and thousands. I'm not sure how much, and I don't think X got his whole share, so he's somewhat put out about it. But he can't say anything out loud, of course. Just threatens."

"And this forger—how does he seem about it? Smug? Repentant? Worried?"

"Not much repentance. He's quite sure he's gotten away with it. Now he seems to think he needs something else like it."

"To keep him at that level. I suppose he still fancies himself a cattle breeder."

"Yes. And he thinks he needs a little more capital to get into it."

"Some men work their way up, but that's hard. Especially if someone's had a taste of the other way. Easy money can ruin a man for doing honest work."

"Money doesn't last very long with him anyway."

"You've told me that before. Maybe he'll go flat, and he'll be easier to deal with."

"He's never easy. He likes to make things difficult for other people. And he's always got something here or there that he can go draw on."

"Well, at the very least it gives you material to work with. I trust this was the business you were referring to the last time I was in town, when you said he'd done some things that were helping you gain strength to resist him."

She nodded.

"Do you think this is something you can use as leverage, the actual information, or more in the line of moral distance, something that gives you justification for separating yourself?"

"Uh!" she said. "I just wish I didn't have to be near him. And his dirty money."

He raised his eyebrows. "It would be good leverage, if you needed it. You say he's afraid of anything getting out."

"He is. But he also says everything is covered up perfectly, and no one could ever prove a thing."

"It would behoove him to tell you that anyway. He doesn't have a compulsion for always telling you the truth, does he?"

"He tells me what he wants and when he wants to, and sometimes things do change from what he tells me and what turns out."

"Well, you never know. I don't like the idea of using leverage myself, but if the time comes around, and let's say you needed to use a lawyer, it's something he might like to have at his disposal. Fight fire with fire."

"I'll keep that in mind."

She put her hand on his, and he could tell she was getting ready to go.

"Don't forget your chalice," he said.

"I won't." She rose and pressed his head against her bosom. "Sir Knight."

The next day, as he rode from the train station in Orin to his home range, he caught the aroma from an alfalfa field in bloom. It reminded him of a woman's perfume—not of a specific perfume that a specific woman wore, but of perfume in general. Overhead the summer sky spread wide and blue, and he felt small but free as he rode along on the bay horse, admiring the single spur he held in his right hand.

In his pasture two days later, as he was climbing the slope after picketing his horses in a fresh area, Lane found a stone. As soon as he saw it, he was compelled to pick it up, though it was not big enough to use for his projects. It was about the size of the heart of a young antelope, and it was shaped somewhat like an actual heart. He held it in his right hand and covered it with his left. It spoke its purpose to him. It could be a rock of trust—she could put her hand on it and tell him things she might not be able to tell him otherwise. Or, she could just put her hand on it without any message. It was Cora's rock.

Lane was the only patron in the small building when the postmaster handed him the letter. He did not recognize the handwriting, cramped and unsteady, and the envelope carried no return address. After breaking it open, he found another envelope inside, one made out of letter-writing paper folded and sealed. He opened it to find a note in Cora's handwriting. It had no salutation or signature, but the contents would have told him the author if the handwriting hadn't.

I am sending you this by way of Mrs. Rutherford. I trust it will arrive safely.

I do not have much time to write, but I wanted to tell you how much I was transported by our last meeting, not to mention the one before that. I cannot tell you how much hope it has given me, to know that you never really gave me up and that you are willing to persevere so that we can be together.

By the way, someone is going to be in Rawlins for a few days beginning Monday next, and if you find it manageable, it would be a convenient time to visit.

Today was Friday. Plenty of time to get things in order.

Lane crested the pine ridge in early morning, riding the bay and leading the sorrel. Until he had a fenced pasture, he had to put up both horses whenever he planned to be gone for very long. Today he chose to skirt Willow Springs, to avoid the public eye. He was carefree; he liked being alone and free on the plains, and he was happy to have the stone in his saddlebags.

When he gave her the rock, she took it in both hands, one on each side, and held it that way.

"I found it in my pasture. When I saw it, I thought I should bring it to you." Having seen that she held it in a different way than he had, he did not want to impose his sense of its purpose.

"What a wonderful thought. It's beautiful. As long as I have it, I'll have a part of you and the place where you are."

She set the stone on the writing table where she had put her handbag when she came in. Now she opened the bag and took out a small package wrapped in red tissue.

"I brought something for you," she said, placing it in his hands.

He sat on the bed, and she sat next to him. With slow, careful movements he unfolded the paper. Within he found a locket, the size that people used for miniature photographs. Expecting to find her picture, he opened it and found a lock of hair bound in thread.

His gaze moved from the object in his hand to her hair where it touched her shoulder. After a moment, he found words.

"I'm stunned. This is incredible. I wish I had had this all that time. It would have been so comforting. I assure you, I would not have touched it when I burned the letters. For which, my apologies once again."

"You've already explained why you felt you had to. It's all right. I understand. But this is different. None of those things are going to happen again." She leaned toward him and kissed him.

When they drew apart, he said, "Would you like a lock of mine?"

"Of course."

"I have a small pair of scissors. We could do it now."

Her face opened in surprise. "You carry scissors?"

"Part of a little sewing kit I carry with me when I travel. Actually I got the idea from some of the punchers on roundup. I bought a little outfit for myself, and I keep it with my traveling things. So we even have a bit of thread to tie it with."

She ran her fingers through his hair. "Made to order."

"It has gray that it didn't have before, and it doesn't grow as thick or fast, but I think we can find a satisfactory chunk. Would you like to do the cutting?"

"Sure."

When she had the little scissors in her hand and was standing in front of him, she asked, "Is there a particular place you would like me to cut from?"

"You choose." He kissed the fabric on the underside of her bosom. "In the French novels, they make a big show of this sort of thing. They cut it as if in defiance of the whole world, and then they take great care to comb over it and hide it. The men collect them in a little souvenir box."

"Well, you're only getting one."

"I don't want any others."

"Where shall I cut it, then?"

"Wherever it's thick enough and long enough."

She found a place on the side, above the back of the ear, and took several small snips. He cut off a length of thread for her, and she tied the lock in a little sheaf. She set it on the table next to the one she had given him, and then she opened her arms to him.

On the train ride north, he took out the locket several times and pondered the lock of hair. Such an odd little thing. Barbers swept up piles of it every day, but a swatch like this, set aside with purpose, was full of meaning. And a lock of hair would last much longer than the body it grew from. Poets wrote about that very idea. A person could burn letters, and it had a purging effect, like getting something out of the blood. But he could not imagine doing anything to a lock of hair. It would violate the sanctity.

He skirted Willow Springs on the way back to his place. A couple of miles from town, he cut across the open plain, adrift again on the sea of grass, moving with the motion of the horse and reliving the golden moments with Cora. A burst of sound from the sky above brought him out of his reverie. He heard it again, an abrupt call and then a trailing off, like *keeerrr*. Looking up, he saw a light-colored hawk, like the one he had seen so long ago carrying a snake. He heard the cry again, and again.

The sounds seemed to come from more than one point. He held up his hand to block out the sun. The birds were hard to pick out, all of them in the vast, blue sky. Then he saw them—four hawks, blondish white, circling high overhead and calling to one another.

At his place once again, he resumed work on the dugout. Spring roundup was over, so he was able to enlist Elbert with a team and wagon to haul the salvage lumber to his site. Then he went to work alone, at his own pace.

He set up two posts for uprights, then a cross-beam and a ridgepole. He used the best boards for the roof, and the next best for the door frame and door. The poorest lumber, warped and cracked, he used to line the walls before he stacked the rocks against them and plastered the gaps with wet clay. After all that, he laid a sheet of canvas over the board roof and thatched the top with black-root sod.

Inside and looking up, he saw that the ridgepole had a sag in it. He went out and scoured the hills until he found a fallen pine that looked sound enough for the task yet light enough to drag with a horse. It took all of a day's labor to trim the log, drag it, cut it for length, and get it forced into place.

For the last step, he mounted the door on the frame, using the leather from an old pair of boots for the hinges. With the door swung inward, he could sit in his entryway and look out upon the world as it stretched away for miles. He had a good vantage point, something to be pleased with. It was a bit primitive, perhaps, more fit for a bachelor than a domestic arrangement, but he would like to share it with Cora all the same. This shelter was nothing like a house that someone could pay to have built, but he was proud of it, crude though it was. He knew she would like it. They could lie in bed together and look out through this doorway, their window on the world.

He opened the locket and gazed at the little shock of hair. He had more of her now than he had ever had before, and it seemed like the promise of things to last. She said she wasn't going to lose him this time.

He touched the hair with his thumb. It was real, part of her, more than a token. It seemed perfectly in place in this unhewn, unpolished, unsettled country. Come live with me and be my love. If love and all the world were young. She would still like it here, with so much to admire.

On the slope below, he could see his two horses grazing. He had grown into this world, quite different from the characters in the novels. Madame Bovary wanted to escape the boredom of the provinces, and Julien Sorel wanted to leave the provinces themselves and go out into the larger world. Lane touched the hair again. This was the opposite. He had come to the provinces and found something to love, something to believe in. Cora. And the natural world that spread out all around him.

Well over a month since he had seen her. They

should be getting back from Missouri about now. He needed to stock up on grub anyway. He could go to town tomorrow.

He found no mail waiting for him at the post office, but he did not let it trouble him. She had a hard time writing with McGee around all the time, and the children were getting older as well. He was not worried. The last time he had been with Cora, she had given herself to him with such abandon that he had no doubt of her intentions. The next time would be the same. Nothing could touch them in the meanwhile.

Joseph Saxton showed his usual reserve as he weighed out the beans, carved off a chunk of bacon, and set the canned goods on the counter.

"How's everything out your way? Haven't seen you for a while."

"Busy. Been working."

"For Nance Fredman again?"

"No, for myself. Building a hut. Far from the madding crowd's ignoble strife."

"Aspiring to be a mute inglorious Milton?"

"No, just his scribe. Or better yet, the amanuensis of time."

Joseph wrapped the bacon in heavy brown paper and tied it with string. "Seems to go by faster every year."

Lane paid for his order and took a sidelong glance at the storekeeper. Joseph usually got in a better last word than that.

With his provisions packed on his saddle, Lane

was still in no hurry to go back to the range. He had not minded the siege alone, but now that he was in town and near other people, he had a yearning for company. When he saw Madeline Edgeworth on the sidewalk near the hotel, he hailed her and invited her to have noon dinner with him.

Their meal being nothing out of the ordinary, they sat at a table in the hotel dining room. Dark-haired Madeline was full of sparkle and self-assurance, as always.

"I haven't seen much of you this summer," she said, tucking in her napkin.

"I've been pretty busy, building a dugout cabin."

"You look like you've been getting sun and exercise."

"Oh, I have been."

The waiter took their order and left.

"And what else is new? They say you go off on jaunts from time to time."

"Who's they?"

"The walls. You know how they talk. And they say you don't always go through town."

"Whew. I might as well be living in a glass house on Main Street."

"We all do."

"And where do the walls say I go?"

Her dark eyes, open and unguarded, met his. "They haven't said it in so many words, but the implication is that you might be going to see someone you knew before."

Lane glanced to either side, then met her gaze. "I might be."

"Well, be careful. You got dropped pretty hard last time."

"I think I have a better chance this time. I think she can summon up what she needs. The fortitude."

"Maybe so. But if you fall into the same pattern as before, you would do well to watch for signs."

He nodded. "Thanks. I'll be on the lookout."

Her mouth changed shape, then was still. "And why aren't you with her right now?"

"She's away."

"With him?"

"Yes. They went back to Missouri. His father is not doing well. The mother is already dead, and he's going back to tend to things."

"The dutiful son."

"Thanks for saying it for me. I imagine he's looking out for his own interests."

She gave a guarded smile. "You know I'm not a great admirer of his. But looking out for oneself, in less contemptible ways, of course, is not a bad practice."

"Well, I'll try not to be the same fool as before." He laughed. "Or a worse one."

"It's good to keep a sense of humor," she said, "but you want to remember, we get one chance at all of it. And that idea isn't original to me, of course."

"Even so, it's a good thing to remember. One chance."

"That's right. Not two. Time goes on."

"I know. Believe me, I know." Sitting across the table from her, he could not ignore her charms.

There had been a time when being away from women for a month left him with low resistance. He had to wonder whether that time would come again. Today he was full of Cora, and although he could resist the dark eyes and full bosom, he could not ignore them.

Hoofbeats behind him on the trail caused him to draw rein and turn around. Here came Elbert, boiling up a cloud of dust on one of the Rosette cow ponies. Lane held the sorrel and waited.

Elbert came to a jolting stop and raised a hand in greeting. "Howdy-do?"

"Afternoon, Elbert. What's in the wind?"

"Seen yuh leavin' town, an' thought Ah could ketch yuh and not have to go all the way out to yer place."

Lane felt his hope rise, as Elbert liked to pick up mail for other people and thus have a reason to stop in at the ranches. "Have you got something for me?"

"Not pursay. But ol' Nance, he told me to let yuh know fall roundup'll be startin' in a week or so, and if yuh want some work, yuh could fall in with us."

"Sounds like a good offer, but I'm not sure I'm in the market for it right now."

"Good enough." Elbert held his head up, as if he was letting the silence hang for a moment. "Had any more trouble?"

"No, I haven't. I've been pretty much keepin' to myself."

"Well, if yuh want to buy a six-gun, let me know. Got an extry one. Traded for it."

"I'll have to think about it. I don't feel that I've got much need for one right now."

"Suit yerself." Elbert gathered his reins. "See yuh later on."

"Same to you, Elbert. Give my best to Nance."

Lane poked along on the sorrel, dragging a length of dead pine at the end of his rope. One of these days, he was going to have to go back to working for wages. If things smoothed out with Cora and he didn't have to be ready to leave at the drop of a hat, he could put in some regular time and build up his stake. He was living cheap, and the dugout had cost him next to nothing, but after another half dozen trips to Laramie, he was going to need to find work. If he ran out of money in the dead of winter, he might wonder about these days when he didn't do much more than marvel at the huge anthills made of twigs, gaze at the clouds, and wait for a letter from Cora.

Right now, with a letter in his pocket, it seemed like time well spent. Eight more days and he'd be in the Crown Hotel again. Four walls and a silken embrace. Meanwhile, he could stock up on firewood and look out for frost. This last good rain and then the warm weather had brought some green back to the range. But the days were getting shorter, and it was time to be drawing things in. He already had the tent stored away in the recess of the dugout. Now he could pile up some firewood, keep his horses well grazed, and think about the buttons on Cora's blouse.

Chapter Thirteen

Lane was studying a pine tree, dead, on the spine of a little ridge, with old weathered roots hanging in a coil where the earth had eroded. Movement down on the plain to the west caught his eye. A horse and rider dipped down into a swale and out of sight for a moment, then rose out of the grass. After another moment, Lane recognized Elbert on the big sorrel he liked to ride when he went across country.

Lane walked down the hill to his camp. His two horses raised their heads and watched as Elbert rode across the hillside toward the dugout. The big sorrel came to a stop, and Elbert stayed on board, resting both hands on the saddle horn. Lane moved around so he wouldn't have to look into the sun as he talked to his visitor.

"Afternoon, Elbert."

"Howdy. Looks like yuh got yer den all finished."

"I think so. It's pretty snug."

"Got a fireplace? Don't see no chimly."

"I'm thinkin' of gettin' a sheet-iron stove for it, for heat and cookin' both."

Elbert nodded as he looked over the structure. "That should do it."

Lane waited for him to say more, but he didn't. "I thought you might have started beef roundup by now."

"Coupla more days, the wagon pulls out. Still got time to make it if yuh want."

"Wish I could, but I've got other irons in the fire right now." Lane waited again, and Elbert still did not speak. "What else is new?"

Elbert lifted his chin and tipped his head to the side. " 'Bout had a little trouble."

"You don't say. Who with?"

"Coupla jaspers had a calf tied up and a little sagebrush fire goin'. Ah come up on 'em, and they took off."

"The hell. Did you keep their rope?"

"Nope. They seen me comin', got their rope off that calf, and hightailed it."

"No idea who they were, huh? Did you throw any lead at 'em?"

"Nah. Too far away." He reached back to his saddlebag on the off side. "But I brung yuh this." He came around with a pistol and holster without a belt.

"Is that the one you told me about?"

"Yep."

"What is it? It doesn't look very big."

"It's a .38, but a man could stop a bull with it if he wanted to." He held it forward.

"I imagine. Nice of you to think of me, but I don't believe I need it."

"Go ahead and take it. Pay me for it later. Even got a few shells." He reached into his vest pocket and pulled out a Bull Durham bag. He tossed it to Lane, who felt the shells move as he caught the bag.

"I don't really need it."

"Just take it. Yuh never know." Elbert glanced at the pile of firewood. "Yuh might get yerself a wood rat."

"Oh, all right. You won't be happy if I don't."

Elbert handed him the gun and holster, then tipped his head in a solid nod. "Can be a good little helper."

Lane smiled. "Everyone doin' his part, to keep the range safe."

A cold, bitter wind was blowing as he walked from the train station to the Crown Hotel. The air didn't smell like rain or snow, either one, but he knew the wintry weather came early to Laramie.

At the hotel, the clerk handed him an envelope, which he said came in earlier in the day. Lane recognized Mrs. Rutherford's handwriting. He put the letter in his pocket, and when he was safe in his room with his bags, he opened it and read it.

Dearest Lane,

Someone has been staying close to home these days and doesn't seem to expect to be gone for about a week. I am sorry I couldn't tell you any sooner. He does have an obligation out of town on the seventh, however. I could see you on that day, but I wouldn't blame you if you didn't want to see me. Nevertheless, I remain hopeful, and I am, as always,

Yours in love,

Cora

Lane felt as if he had been kicked in the chest by a horse. After coming all this way, even checking for mail in Willow Springs, and then to be met with this—it was not quite the same as being stood up, but a big emptiness nonetheless. He assured himself that things weren't over, that he would see her again, but here he was, shut out and alone. After reading the letter three, four times, he developed an irritation at the helpless tone. Nothing she could do about it. Just go along, then apologize. Yours in love. Sometimes. Well, he didn't have much choice. He would catch the train back tomorrow. Leave a note in the meanwhile, agree to come back on the seventh. *Don't be the weak one.*

When he arrived in Laramie on the seventh, he went to a café, having decided not to take a room first. He wrote a note and sent it to her by way of the washerwoman. In less than an hour, Cora arrived. She was wearing the blouse with dark blue buttons, which matched a medicine bottle he had seen in a shop window a while earlier. As she came closer, he saw the apologetic look, like a dog waiting to be cuffed.

"I'm so glad you came," she said, pressing close to him.

"I decided not to take a room until I saw you and knew that things weren't going to go up in a wisp of smoke again."

"I'm sorry. I'm so sorry." She met his eyes, and he saw a desperate look. "You can come to my house," she said. "Someone is gone, and the children are at a show."

A strange feeling passed through him, as if he felt a gun barrel at the back of his head. Her daring surprised him, but the dread prevailed. "I'd rather take a room."

She stood back half a step. "Whatever you want. I'll give you time to get checked in, and then I can meet you there."

She met him at the Crown, as arranged. As soon as the door closed behind her, he took her in his arms and said, "What happened last time?"

"Just love me. Take me and love me, and we can talk about everything else later."

When the tension was spent and they lay propped up on elbows facing one another, he came back to the question.

"So what happened? What's this fellow up to? Is he hanging around the house because he suspects something, or is he hiding from the people he swindled?"

She seemed to sulk a little at being interrogated. "Oh, he goes out."

"You said in the note that he didn't."

"He's been staying pretty close to home, but he does go out sometimes."

"Was he sitting in your lap that day, then?"

She demurred. "Well, actually, we weren't at home when I wrote the letter, or at least right after I wrote it, but the children were, with a woman who was taking care of them, and it would have been far too confusing for you to have come this far to find that out by word of mouth through Mrs. Rutherford, so I tried to make it simple."

"Did you go somewhere with him, then?"

Her voice was more assertive now. "Well, yes. We went somewhere."

"Something you couldn't tell me at the time?"

"I thought I could explain it easier, later."

He exhaled. "All right."

She took a deep breath and started in. "It happened on the spur of the moment. Someone decided that we needed to go away for a few days, just the two of us. He said we were going to Denver. I knew you were already on the way down, and there was nothing I could do, except get a letter to Mrs. Rutherford on the way out of town. That in itself was a contrivance."

Lane felt a tightening in his stomach. "Was this his idea of a romantic getaway?"

"He said we need to be together."

"And you didn't feel you could do anything but go along."

"I don't know how I could have told him I

wouldn't. And I guess he deserved a chance, at least, to try to do something right."

"My God, how many chances does he get? How long are you going to continue going along with this fellow's whims? I thought you were going to put some distance between you and him."

"I intend to."

"Intend. That puts everything in the future. You told me six months ago that you thought you could see your way to getting free, and I'm wondering when you might do it."

Her sulking had passed into a vacant expression. "I don't know."

"You do intend to get away from this fellow, don't you?"

"That's what I've said."

"I know you've said it, but saying and doing are two different things." He caught himself. "Look, I don't want to be telling you what to do with your life, but since it's keeping me on the edge of my seat, I think I have a right to ask if you plan to make a separation, and if so, when."

"I don't know."

"You don't know the if, or you don't know the when?"

"I just don't know."

"Well, let's back up. In what frame of mind did you go on this little trip with him? Was it a holiday for you?"

"In a way it was, or it could have been, if it hadn't been for what I knew I was doing to you. But my frame of mind, as you put it, was that I couldn't see how I could do anything else."

He thought he grasped it then—the thing he had read about, of all places, in a French novel. He remembered the phrase "craven submissiveness," describing the way a woman would appease her husband and punish herself for her adultery. Then, having submitted, she had made recompense and could go back to her lover.

Maybe there were two of her after all, as she had suggested long ago. The trouble was, they weren't separate entities like Rachel and Leah; and there wasn't any guarantee he would get one, even the less desirable one, if he waited seven years.

"This fellow must be pretty good," he said.

"In what way?"

"He seems to know exactly when to pull the rug out from under you. Did you do something to tip him off?"

"I don't think so."

"Maybe it's something he can sense. Some men claim to be able to tell when a woman is ready. Almost as if they could sniff it. Maybe he can sense your anticipation."

"I don't know."

"Neither do I. For all I know, someone warned him. I did go through town that day, specifically to see if there was any mail that would signal a change in plans. His stool pigeon could have seen me packed for travel and then sent a telegram. Did he spring it on you that same day?"

"Yes."

"Well, however he does it, he seems pretty good

at it. It's too bad you can't mount a little more resistance, especially with these other things he's pulled. You yourself said you didn't like living with a thief and his tainted money."

"I don't."

"Well, I wish you weren't so powerless to do something about it, unless you'd rather be with him to begin with."

She began to sob.

"Look, I'm not trying to make you cry. I love you. It's just that I have to look out for myself, and not go on like this forever."

She sobbed louder, and when she raised her head she had tears in her eyes. "Oh, Lane, I hate myself for what I do to you. I'm no good. You should just go away. Forget about me."

He put his hand on her waist. "I can't do that."

"You should. I'm no good."

"Oh, there's nothing wrong with you that can't be fixed, if you could get away from this fellow that keeps you knuckled under."

"I don't know why you ever wanted me."

"Because I love you. Of course."

"I don't know why. You shouldn't. I've never been any good, since long before I met you."

"Oh, come on, darling. Deep down, you're a good person, if you could get out of this situation where you feel you have to lie all the time."

"No, I'm not. I'm worse than you know. I'm an adulteress, a liar, a thief, and worse than that."

"Well, now, that's rather harsh. Why do you call yourself a thief? For abetting him?"

"No," she said, her face contorted with pain. "I've stolen, too. I took some of his ill-gotten money, and I used it to rent another place where I was hoping to go live. But it all fell apart. He followed me there, and he made me come back."

"That doesn't seem like a pure case of theft, but if you feel wrong about using stolen money, I've got to agree with you in part, at least." Then he added, "What about him following you there? That doesn't sound very good."

"It's not."

"Did he do something to you there?"

"He wanted to poison the place. Ruin it for me."

"He did something."

"He wanted to make me feel worthless there."

"Like he did in the empty house."

She did not answer right away. When she did, she said, "Yes."

Lane hesitated. "Has he done this in any other places?"

She didn't answer.

"Perhaps it's none of my business, but it does seem to go beyond the customary privileges."

After another period of silence, she said, "It's ugly. He wants me to feel ugly. And no good."

"Has he made a pattern of doing it?"

"He's done it to me in every house we've lived in, plus the two places I mentioned, and a couple of others that don't matter."

"And he does this for punishment, when he thinks you need to be brought into line?"

"That seems to be it."

"Then at other times, all he has to do is give you a look that says, 'I could do something, but I won't,' and you go along."

She didn't say anything.

"So this is what makes you worse than a liar and a thief?"

"No," she said, shaking her head in an air of resignation. "No, I've done worse."

"Well, if you think you can talk about it, I'll be willing to listen."

"I don't know. I'll have to think about it."

Lane didn't speak for a moment. Then he said, "What other kinds of things has this fellow done?"

"Oh, you name it."

"You told me one time you didn't think he'd ever done anything with other women. Do you still believe that, or is it the sort of thing you think you're supposed to believe?"

"Probably the latter."

"I don't think his kind would feel in control if he didn't do something on the side. Of course he would never tell you, especially when he knows there's something he can act superior to. 'I would never do to you what you did to me.' Something like that."

She was calmer now. "I don't know how far he's gotten, but I don't think he's as pure as he lets on. He has at least attempted." After a pause, she added, "My sister told me he tried something with her."

"Alice."

"Yes, Allie. You remembered. Well, she came to stay with me when I had Franklin. Then when I had Belinda, she said she couldn't come, and it wasn't until years later that I found out why."

"Pleasant chap."

"Let's not talk about him. Just hold me."

He took her in his arms, but she did not relax. He felt as if she was staring over his shoulder. They lay there, tense, for several minutes until he spoke.

"I don't know if there's something you want to say."

"I don't either. You got me started, and there are other things that I've never told anyone and wish I could."

"These are the things that are worse?"

"It's really one thing, and it's so hideous. I'm afraid that if I tell you, you'll never love me again."

"Oh, I don't care what it is. I'll still love you." He kissed her, and they drew apart.

"And you won't tell anyone?"

"I promise."

"I need to tell someone."

"Go ahead. It's safe with me."

"You won't do anything with it?"

"No. If it's that private, I'll respect it."

She lay on her back, her eyes directed at the ceiling. "This is a terrible story, and until now, there have been only two people who have known about it. McGovern, as you call him, and me."

He gave her hand a pat of assurance.

"As I told you before, I met him in Nebraska. He was doing land work near where I lived. We met, and from the beginning he seemed to have a power over me. He was tall, and handsome, and he took authority. He would tell me when he wanted to see me, where to meet him, and the like. Sometimes I had to make up stories for my parents, but I did what I thought I was supposed to do—take orders from a man, just as I had seen my mother do. So I met him, and when I did, he told me what to do."

"How old were you?"

"About sixteen. He was the first one I did anything with. When I did, he told me I was his. Sometimes it scared me, but I knew I was pleasing him, so I gave myself to him whenever he wanted me to and I could manage it." She hesitated, then picked up. "And of course, within a few months I could tell I was going to have a baby."

Lane frowned as he did the figuring. Franklin wouldn't be that old.

She let out a sigh toward the ceiling. "I was afraid. I didn't know if I wanted to have his baby, to have that bond between us. I didn't know if I wanted to be his already, forever. I waited as long as I could, and then I told him. I told him about the baby, and how I felt."

She paused, and he patted her hand.

"He had been drinking, and he went into a rage. We were in his room, and I was afraid someone would hear. He shouted, 'You don't want my baby! You don't want my baby!' He started pounding me with his fists on my stomach, again and again."

"My God."

"Then I cried for a long time, and he sat in the chair drinking until he said he couldn't take any more and went out. I started bleeding. It was terrible. I took the sheets off the bed and folded them into a pad, to absorb as much of it as I could. Then I lost it—the baby, everything. It was far enough along to recognize what it was. It was a baby."

Her face was twisted in agony now, and he knew she could not be making up the story.

"I was half the night going through it, with him off who knows where. Then I cleaned things up as well as I could, wrapped up the bundle, and left. I had miles to walk that night, and I didn't know what to do with the thing I was carrying. When I came to the canal, I tore off some strips, tied up the bundle, and threw it in the water. My dead baby floated away, and I sneaked back home. I don't know how I walked that far, but I did. I was in bed for almost a week."

"Did he come to check on you?"

"No, he stayed away. When I was up and about again, he found out from Allie, and then he came around."

"Was he repentant?"

"He acted as if nothing had happened. I told him, of course, and he said nothing at all."

Lane let out a long breath. "And in spite of all this, you went ahead and married him."

"Not for a couple of years, but yes."

"So the thing that might have given you a reason to break with him didn't work that way at all. Almost to the contrary."

"It would seem that way."

Lane rolled his eyes. "And in the years that have passed, have you ever talked about it?"

"Very seldom."

"And what does he say when it comes up?"

Her voice was cold. "He says it would be a terrible thing for someone to find out about me."

"About you? What about him?"

"He likes to point out that I did it all on my own, without consulting anyone."

"What cheek! How absolutely brazen. He's at least an accessory after the fact, not to mention a woman-beater to begin with, and he walks out on you when you're at your worst. You could have died. Then he thinks he can hold it over you. Huh. You say no one has ever known about it except for you and him. What became of the bundle?"

"That's the worst part. Some poor farmer fished it out of a headgate. It was the talk of the valley for weeks, how someone could do something like that. And I've lived in shame ever since. I don't know how a person could do worse."

"Well, it's not a good thing to have done, but you were young and bewildered and on your own. I don't blame you, given the circumstances. And you sure didn't choose to miscarry it." He paused. "It's probably good for you to tell someone, and it might even help if you told someone else. At any rate, I don't think you should take all the blame yourself."

"Well, I did it."

"All the same, this fellow doesn't seem to have much of a conscience about it. It seems as if he's pushed it all off on you."

"That's his specialty. Blame everything on me, and I'm willing to take it."

"Well, you two sure found each other." He caught himself. "I wonder if there's some way we can use this to break his power over you."

She laid her hand on his arm and turned her eyes toward him. "Please, Lane, you said you wouldn't do anything with it."

He swallowed. "It's not like I'm going to go tell a sheriff. But this is a powder keg, if you want to use it to shake his grip on you."

"I wish you wouldn't, Lane. That's not why I told you. I couldn't risk anyone knowing about this. Except you. I trust you. But if this got out, and my own children ever found out about it—"

Lane did not answer. He just ran it through his head. Ancient evil. Secrets based on shame. The type of thing that should work like dynamite, but the shame made it work like glue. As long as it worked that way, beyond her control, he wasn't sure how much he could do to counteract it. He could counterweigh it with their own love, but he couldn't clean it out.

She was resting now, with her eyes closed. He could tell that going through the story had exhausted her. Her eyelids and eyelashes looked so pretty, so innocent. He tried to picture her as a girl, before she met her master. Young and appealing, ready to be taken. His own phrase came to him. They sure found each other.

In spite of her submissiveness, though, she had her daring. She always did. He wondered about her offer to take him to her house, whether it was a way to trump the master in his lair or, more likely, a way of proving something to herself and of showing her lover how far she was willing to go. Maybe it was a kind of compensation. He couldn't remember the precise sequences of that earlier era, but it seemed that sometimes, after leaving him in the dark, she had come back with more initiative than usual. Seeing things that way, he couldn't escape the conclusion that the way she treated him was the mirror image, or reverse, of the way she treated her husband.

So pretty with her eyes closed, and such good intentions. Best to make the most of the opportunity, anyway. Seize the day. As he drew close to her and kissed her, she opened her eyes and took him in her arms. His boldness came to him, and he merged with the silken center of the world.

As soon as he came over the ridge with the two horses, he knew something was wrong. He could smell something charred. As his camp came into view, he saw what it was. Someone had pulled down his work.

Boards and sod from the roof lay in a heap of rubble with dirt and rocks from the walls. Whoever had done the damage had yanked out the center support pole, the ridgepole, the uprights, and the crossbeam. All of the big pieces had been dragged to the fire pit and set on fire. He recognized the unburned ends of all the pieces he had worked with. Nothing salvageable there. Half his firewood was gone, too. They had used it to get the big fire going.

This was what he got, and it wasn't the work of Elbert's phantom rustlers. It was someone who knew him, someone who watched his movements and knew when he was going to be away for a couple of days. He didn't have to guess very much. Either one man or two.

He stripped the two horses and set them out to graze. Then he sorted through the remains of his dugout. Whoever had done it had seen fit to pull out the timbers and burn them rather than try to burn a structure that was over half dirt and rock. The good part of that method was that the belongings inside were still intact. That included his tent, tucked away in the cavelike recess in the back wall, plus the six-shooter and shells stowed inside the rolled-up canvas.

He took out the little Bull Durham sack and counted the shells. Twelve. He counted out six, loaded the pistol, and went to the rubbish heap to pick out a can. At the base of the cream-colored bluffs, with the cool autumn breeze sifting through the pines at his back, he took his shots. It was not a good way to think. He liked the muscle in his arm better, but he didn't know how far someone else might want to go.

CHAPTER FOURTEEN

Lane sorted through the rubble and wreckage. He knew the destruction was meant to demoralize him, and he couldn't keep it from having that effect. Nevertheless, he focused on the work itself and kept himself occupied. The lumber he thought he might be able to use again went into one stack, while the broken and splintered pieces went to the woodpile. He separated the rocks into three groups according to relative size, and he shoveled the dirt and sod into two large mounds. Still undecided as to whether he should attempt another shelter before the cold weather set in, he sat at the entryway of his tent and looked out over the country.

This one disaster, although it undid days and weeks of his labor, did not change much. The land remained the same—endless miles of rangeland rolling out across hills and buttes and mesas. If a cabin fell in, a horse broke its leg, or a man died, the big country lived on. Right now it was getting ready for winter.

He didn't know if he wanted to try living in a tent all winter. He had heard that the storms hung on this ridge, and from the size and plentitude of pine trees, he could tell the snow piled up deep, especially here on the north side.

He weighed the options. He could try building another shelter, either a dugout or a shack, but then he would be too worried to leave it for very long. That would be playing right into the adversaries' methods. He could spend a while in a line shack, doing a bit of lookout work for Nance if the old man wanted some done. Or he could pack up everything, shake the dirt out of his books and clothes one more time, and find a town to winter in. Whatever the case, he wasn't going to decide today. He could let things sift for a few days rather than react when his spirits were at a low ebb. Meanwhile, he wouldn't say anything to anybody.

Within a week, he received a letter from Cora. It came by way of Mrs. Rutherford, and it was short and unsigned. She invited him to come visit on the twenty-first. Today was the nineteenth. He would have to go. He didn't like to leave his camp alone, but as long as Cora could see him, he needed to see her. Maybe he could push things along as well.

On the twentieth he cut cross-country, skirting town by several miles. He stabled the horses and caught the train as usual, then settled in for the long ride. With the days getting shorter, the train rolled into Laramie at dusk. He sent a message to Mrs. Rutherford and tried to relax in his room.

The next morning at about ten, the clerk knocked on his door. The lady was downstairs and would like to visit with him there. Lane tipped the clerk, waited a long minute, and went down the staircase.

Cora was wearing a very dark blue wool dress and matching jacket. She looked reserved but not defensive as she rose to take his hand.

"Did you not want to come up? It's easier to talk there."

"I've only got a few minutes."

"Oh. I thought he was going to be gone. Is he leaving later in the day?"

She hesitated. "He changed his plans. He says he's not going until tomorrow. He just told me at breakfast."

"Rather a habit of his, it seems."

"I suppose." Her downcast expression had returned. "Do you think you could stay another day?"

"I can stay as long as you want, but I would hope we were making some progress."

"I know. You made that clear last time."

He weighed his thoughts for a moment and then said, "When do you think you might do something?"

She brought her gaze up and fixed her eyes on him. "Actually, I have."

"Really? What did you do?"

"I've been to see a lawyer. He's going to work on a separation."

"You don't seem to be very happy about it."

"It's not easy."

"I don't suppose so."

"Anyway, I wanted to be able to tell you in person. I'm sorry I can't visit longer today, but I'll try to make up for it tomorrow."

"I always have a good idea how. But you seem to be rather down about things."

"Say what you will about him, it's a marriage, and one doesn't walk away from it all that easily."

He studied her sad countenance. "I'm trying to understand that. But you have plenty of justification."

"I know."

"And I hope that in the process, your lawyer can bring out some of that. Have you told him about this fellow's maneuvers?"

"Not yet."

"I trust you will."

"I don't know how much I can tell him. Some of it is so—private."

"The last time I was here, you gave me to understand that he's committed some rather atrocious acts, and I gather that you've never really held him to account on any of them, or even on lesser things such as plundering your private reserves. You haven't, have you?"

"No, not really."

"Well, you have the chance now. You can have someone else do it for you. It's just a matter of giving him the ammunition."

"I'll see how he wants to do it."

"What's this lawyer's name, anyway?"

"Wood. Charles Wood."

"Hmm."

"I believe he has a brother who has a ranch up your way."

"That may be where I heard the name. Well, I hope he's good at what he does."

"He should be." Cora glanced at the clock behind the desk. "I need to be going."

He took her hands again and kissed her. "I'm glad we got to visit this much. And I look forward to tomorrow."

"So do I. I'm glad you can stay over another day. I'm sorry about today, and I'll try to be more cheerful."

"It's all right. Like I say, don't apologize. Just do something."

"I am."

"Until tomorrow, then?"

"Yes. Look for me at about this same time."

Midmorning came around the next day. Lane began watching the clock at about nine, and by eleven he could recognize the old familiar feelings of anxiety—a nervous stomach, a restlessness in the legs, an occasional sharp pain deep inside. He wanted to go out and walk off some of the nervousness, but if he did, he would miss her. Even if she came by just long enough to schedule something for the next day, he wanted to be there.

By one o'clock she had still not appeared, nor had she sent a message. He fretted with the persistent worry that she might not show at all, that she might have been detained or worse. Happen what may, he was going to have to try to resolve something, so he took the room for another night. A quick summing up of expenses told him he could not make many more trips like this one.

At two o'clock he decided he had to get out of the room for a while. Leaving word with the hotel clerk that he would be back in an hour, he went out to walk the streets. Cold, damp weather was building, and he walked at a brisk pace. He did not go near her house, but he went up and down several residential streets and at length yielded to the temptation of knocking on Mrs. Rutherford's door.

It was opened by a thin, haggard, gray-haired woman who did not have the appearance of having found much in life to enjoy.

"Yes, sir?"

"Excuse me, but are you Mrs. Rutherford?"

"That I am."

"I'm sorry to trouble you, but my name is Lane Weller. Friend of Cora."

"Oh, yes. What do you need?"

"She didn't make it for an appointment earlier in the day, and I was afraid something might have happened. I was wondering if you might know anything."

"No, I don't know nothin'." Her voice had a whine to it, a tone he had heard in people who never seemed to be free of the effects of drink, even when they were dry.

He cleared his throat. "I was wondering if there might be a way to find out. If it's not too much trouble—"

The whining voice came louder now. "Well, isn't that fine? Your man of leisure wants an answer. Got nothin' better to do than to go causin' trouble in other people's lives. Some folks has to work, but it appears some don't. They've got time to send workin' people on errands. People that have to work for what they've got."

"I'm sorry for the trouble, then. But if a message did happen to come, I'm in the usual place."

"The Crown."

"Yes."

"Well enough. The gentleman is at the Crown. I'll pass it on."

"Thank you."

Cold rain was drizzling down by the time he reached the awning of the hotel. With no messages at the desk, he went up to his room.

Quite a surprise with the washerwoman. He doubted she spewed out that sort of resentment at the people who paid her. Perhaps he should have given her something, but contrary to her impressions, he didn't have money to toss around.

Four o'clock came, then five. At half past six, when he had given up all hope of seeing her that day, a knock came at the door. He opened it to find the clerk holding a wrinkled envelope.

Steeled but shaking, he sat in the chair and opened the letter. It bore no salutation or closing, but the writing was Cora's. The note was brief, saying that someone was home and his presence was keeping her from going out.

Prisoner in her own house. The master must

have gotten up that morning, yawned and stretched, and declared he wasn't going anywhere. That was apparently all it took. Lane could imagine her moving about the house in a mute, servile manner. Maybe a timorous suggestion. I think I'd like to go out for a bit. Oh, you don't need to.

Well, by God, he himself was not a prisoner—not to the same degree, anyway. He put on his hat and overcoat and went out to walk the streets some more.

Dark had fallen, and the cold rain was turning to slushy snow. He needed to burn off the nervousness. He walked and walked, paying little attention to houses or businesses but having the general sense that normal people were inside, dry and warm, conducting normal lives. At one corner he stepped into the street and was almost struck by a carriage that went by. He hadn't heard the horses or seen the lamps. As the vehicle passed, he saw the shades drawn and a glow behind them.

He dared to walk past her house, which he found dark in the front but light in back. He imagined her serving supper to the master, who might toss off a comment about the weather and leave the rest to be understood.

Even without Madeline's warning, he would have seen that things had come around to the familiar patterns. He was shut out again, feeling like an outcast in the dark. His relation with Cora had reached another deadlock. Cora said she was the same person as before, and he believed her. The only thing different was that he understood things better now, or at least thought he did.

In the morning he went back out into the chilly gray world and found the office of Charles Wood. There was dynamite to be had, and it might be just the thing for this logjam.

Lane found the lawyer alone in his office, seated at a large oak desk. At the entrance of the visitor, Mr. Wood closed a cream-colored folder and set a capped bottle of ink on it. He sat back from the desk with his hands resting on the edge. A middle-aged man, thinning on top and gone to gray on the sides, clean-shaven and jowly, he looked as if he could hold his own against a platter of pork chops or a dish of bread pudding. He wore a pair of spectacles that magnified his eyes and gave him an owlish look.

"Yes, sir. How can I help you?"

"My name is Lane Weller, and I come to intercede on behalf of a person who I believe is a client of yours."

"And that person might be—?"

"Cora McGavin."

"I represent both Mr. and Mrs. McGavin in their various interests."

"I see."

Mr. Wood made a slight nod for him to continue.

"I understand that Mrs. McGavin has recently spoken with you."

"I couldn't say how recently. That is, I wouldn't."

"I see. To rephrase it, I should say that I understand Mrs. McGavin is initiating some action to separate herself from her husband, and I might have some information that could help advance the purpose."

The lawyer put his fingertips together and settled his hands on the crest of his waistcoat. "Mr. Weller, first let me say that your name is not unknown to me. Second, let me tell you that I do not discuss my clients' affairs with someone who comes in off the street."

"Even if someone offers you information that might help you in a proceeding?"

"Mr. Weller, I don't know what proceeding you might be referring to."

"Why, Mrs. McGavin's attempt to get free of her husband."

"If there were such a proceeding under way, I would not discuss it with you. Since there isn't, I don't mind telling you that much."

"Then you are not representing Mrs. McGavin in any kind of separation."

"I have told you that much."

A dizziness came over him, and he felt as if he were drifting. The lawyer's voice brought him back.

"Anything else?"

"I don't think so. I'm sorry for the misunderstanding. I had the impression that she was being held in a situation against her will."

"Say nothing of it. My work is filled with misunderstanding. But a word to the wise. If Mrs. McGavin chooses to stay in a situation, it is not against her will. And your efforts might be better employed elsewhere."

"Thank you."

"Don't mention it." The lawyer directed his gaze at the ink bottle and moved his hand across the desk.

Lane took the action as his cue and walked back out into the cold day.

In his room again, he let the undeniable truth sink in. She had lied to him, and she had done so to string him along, not to make things easier on either of them. It shook all the faith he had in her. The code between clandestine lovers was supposed to be that they did not lie to each other. Either of them might deceive a spouse, but they were supposed to be true to each other. That was the noble view. The common one, which he had heard around campfires and in saloons, was that if she lied to one man, she would lie to another. As Lane put it in his own terms, she treated him as she did her husband. That was a hard pill. It had no saving irony, no poetic paradoxes as in "When my love swears that she is made of truth, I do believe her, though I know she lies." The blunt truth kept coming back: He, who had been lied about, had now been lied to.

He told himself two things, and he did not know if he could adhere to either of them. For one, he was not going to stay another night in Laramie on this trip. For another, he was not going to leave until he could see her and sort out at least some of the tangle. To follow through, he could not wait passively.

He wrote a note and sent it, with a dollar, to Mrs. Rutherford for delivery. Its message was simple.

If you do not come to see me by noon, I will go to your house and we can settle things by confrontation.

An hour and a half later, she was sitting in the chair in his room. She was wearing the blouse with the dark blue buttons; her eyes, full of apprehension, matched the color.

"I just walked out. I'm going to have some answering to do when I get back, but here I am for the moment."

"Does he still act as if there's nothing to lift a finger about?"

"As far as what he says, yes."

"So if he can keep you from bringing anything out in the open, he can laugh in your face. You don't dare do anything but lie."

"That's not entirely true. I stand up to him on some things. We have our disputes."

"But not on anything major, such as this."

Her eyes fell. "Not yet."

"Cora, I don't want to put you in a position where you have to lie to me. Anymore."

She looked up. "What do you mean?"

"I talked to the attorney, Mr. Wood, and I understand that there's nothing under way."

She did not answer, and her eyes would not meet his.

"I have to tell you I found it very discouraging. It wasn't as if it were something you said to placate me, some passive half-truth. It was outright."

"I wanted to," she sobbed. "I tried to put myself up to it, but I couldn't. Every time I try to build up the courage, he wears me down and I can't follow through. It's like you said, as if he can sense it in me."

"And all he has to do is hover over you?"

"Something like that."

He let out a long breath and picked himself up. "Cora, there's plenty of fight left if you want to try. You've got his fraud and embezzlement, and a long history of . . . cruelty, bodily harm. You could break his power. All you have to do is want to."

Tears were splashing on her skirt. "I can't. I've tried, and I just can't. I get determined, and then I go limp as a rag. I'm weak. I told you I was no good, and I'm not."

He took her hand. "I don't want to hold it against you, but I must say I had the wind quite knocked out of me when I talked to your lawyer. What were you hoping to gain with that story?"

"I don't know. I panicked. I didn't want to lose you. When I lost you before, I felt I had nothing to rely on. Nothing solid in this world. I can't tell you how dark it got. I would be cleaning house, or washing clothes, and all of a sudden it would come down on me. Total despair. I didn't want to go through that again. I felt I had to keep you."

"And yet you put me on a level with your husband. Someone to lie to. What better way to lose me?" An idea flashed. "Of course, you'll never lose him that way. He likes you to lie to him. It gives him a hold over you."

"I'm sorry. I told you I was a liar. I've lied for so long, day in and day out, that I don't know the difference. It's like his stealing. It's all become too easy."

"As easy as lying, as the line goes. But you don't have to live that way. You can build yourself back up if you want."

She shook her head. "He told me once, after you and I had started seeing each other again, but before I think he had a glimmering, that he didn't burn all the letters. He said he kept two, apparently very revealing ones, and he has them to show if I ever went to court."

"Get them back. They're not his. Tell this fellow Wood you want them."

"I think Mr. Wood has them."

Lane exhaled. "That makes sense. He said he'd heard my name before. But that doesn't mean he's actually got the letters. It could be a bluff on McGee's part."

"It could be."

"I'll tell you, this is a real peach you're married to. A complete blackmailer on top of everything else. Do you want to live like that for the rest of your life?"

"No, I don't. When I'm with you, I feel built up. I've got courage, I've got determination. But when

I'm back under his—influence, I guess—I go weak. I turn to mush." Her eyes met his again. "I *am* weak. I hate myself for lying to you. And if I can't treat you any better than that, I don't deserve you."

"But you want me."

She smiled. "That's never changed."

"My lovely Cora." He kissed her. "What do you think you want to do, then?"

"Everything you say is true. I just haven't been able to make myself go through with it. I can try it one more time. Will you let me?"

"Oh, please don't ask me what I'll let you do. I'll go along with it. One more try. But I want a time limit."

"Two weeks?"

"Good enough. I'll be back in town in two weeks. If you could see me today, you can see me then."

He found his camp unbothered since he had seen it last. The objects inside his tent had a strange immobility to them, but once he started unpacking his bags, the place became a dwelling again.

Back to the routine of living in the breaks, he had to resume thinking about the winter ahead. Part of it would depend upon what happened with Cora. One way or the other, he didn't have the money to buy lumber. Even one more trip to Laramie was going to cut into what little he had left. He was going to have to find work. If by some good turn of events she was able to get free of her jailer, he could try to find work in Laramie or Cheyenne. Winter there, and see what came next. If nothing happened, he could buy a little sheepherder's stove, hunt coyotes, and see about picking up some work with Nance. In past years, Nick stayed on the payroll all winter. Maybe Elbert was moving into that position. The right-hand man. Hunt coyotes, then. Figure something out.

That was the way things were with Cora, always up in the air. He could have gotten in at least some work this season if he hadn't been keeping himself available. Well, he was going to have to change that pattern.

At the end of a week's time he decided to go into Willow Springs to check for mail and buy a few supplies. As he was getting ready to go, he saw the opportunity to shoot a deer. A band of four of them appeared on a slope, about half a mile downhill. He took out his rifle, made a good sneak, and killed a medium-sized buck with forked horns. After dressing the animal, he went for the horses. By the time he got the deer skinned, quartered, and packed, the sun had crossed the high point. He still had time for a trip to town, and he ought to be able to get something for the fresh meat.

Curley the trader, always in the mood for bartering, gave him a side of bacon, a box of rifle shells, and a pair of wool gloves in exchange for the meat. Counting himself ahead on the day, in spite of another hour spent, Lane went about his errands. By the time he had checked at the post office and bought some canned goods from Joseph Saxton, the sun was beginning to slip in the west.

At the prospect of going back to his camp alone, after finding no mail and having only superficial contact with people in town, he felt an emptiness setting in. He thought he might like the reasonable conversation of another person, plus the insight of a woman. On a hunch he went into the hotel, and after the preliminary courtesies with Rox Barlow, he sent a note up to Madeline Edgeworth, inviting her to an early supper. She sent back word of acceptance, saying she would come down in about a quarter of an hour.

When she appeared, Lane was impressed by her calm, assured manner. She was dressed for cool weather, in a wine-colored wool dress and jacket, all neat. Her dark hair was pinned back, and her eyes sparkled. She carried a soft aroma of powder and perfume, and her hand felt gentle as she gave it to him in greeting.

"Lane Weller, man of the lonesome range," she said, smiling.

"Madeline Edgeworth, woman of charm and wisdom."

She laughed and went before him as they found their way to a table. When they were seated, she gave a half smile and said, "What's new in your adventures?"

"Perhaps you could tell me. I learn all about myself when I come to town."

"I don't believe I've heard anything new on you. Is there?"

"One little thing, and I wouldn't expect anyone to have mentioned it. You're the first person I've told." He looked around the room and then spoke in a lowered voice. "Parties unknown came and wrecked my dugout cabin while I was off on a visit."

She gave a look of displeasure. "That doesn't sound good."

"No, it's not."

"I would guess you see some connection between the two events."

"It's hard not to. I've had trouble with these two fellows all along, and I'm pretty sure they're in communication with old what's-his-name."

"Oh, yes. Him. She's still with him, I take it."

"I'm sorry to say she is."

"And you?"

"I'm waiting to see if she can get away. Sometimes I feel as if I'm playing the seven-year stall."

"Oh, it's hard, once he's got her trained that well."

"She tries, and she just can't marshal her forces."

Madeline gave him a silent look. "She says she can't. Those are her words, aren't they?"

"Yes, but I believe her."

"Of course you do. But even if it seems he's got complete control over her—has her trained, as I said—she still has some choice in the matter."

He brightened. "You know, I've heard that last part somewhere before."

Madeline smiled. "You may hear it again, but probably not from her."

"She's too busy trying to get her head above water. She comes up, and he dunks her again. And she goes along with it."

"Well, I've given you my opinion on him before. It's a mystery why women cling to someone like that. I think it takes a certain kind."

"That's my interpretation. They match all too well."

"Probably so. Sometimes I wonder why you've put up with as much as you have. But I think I understand."

"Go ahead."

"You're a fool. The best kind. You're stuck on her. You love her beyond any sense or reason in the world."

"That much is true. I've been willing to take the big chance, and if that means enduring a little torment, why, what the hell? The world doesn't owe me anything. I don't have any God-given right to get what I want just because I want it. I would be willing to take my knocks and start over even if I didn't bring it on myself. And I did, or at least a great part of it, so I don't have any complaint."

"The best kind. No wonder she loves you. But I still think you're throwing yourself away. You're still young, though, and I'm not afraid for you having to start over."

"You think that's where I'm headed?"

"I'll put it this way, not in terms of you. If she hasn't left him by now, I don't think she will."

"I'm trying to resist that wisdom, but I have a nagging sense . . ."

"That I might be right."

"Yes, and I haven't heard it from anyone else."

Dusk had fallen when Lane paid for dinner and went out to find his horses. As he stepped past the light cast through the dining room windows, he looked into a dark recessed doorway to adjust his eyes. When he brought his gaze out to the sidewalk again, he saw Quist leaning against the building up ahead, smoking his pipe.

Lane walked past the hitching rail where his horses were tied. As he took the next few paces, he felt himself tensing.

Quist stood up straight and took the pipe from his mouth.

Lane spoke to break the silence. "Well, if it isn't the fellow who kicked me in the head."

"What of it? I think you understood why."

"Seems like you're dogging me again. Always on the lookout, aren't you?"

"I go where I want."

"Maybe you do, but you've crossed my path more times than I've cared for."

"I thought maybe you'd learn to take it. That's what your kind does. Sneak around, and then take what you get for it."

"I'm through taking it. From the likes of you, and from the likes of the man whose ass you kiss."

"You're talking strong today."

"So are you, for not having the company of your pal."

"Aw, go on. I can take care of myself with some

dude like you. Go pick some flowers, or write a poem. Hope some girl can sneak out and meet you in the willows."

Lane felt the muscle in his arm as he punched Quist once, twice, three times. The pipe went clattering on the sidewalk, and the man slumped against the building. Lane grabbed him by the jacket, slammed him into the building twice, and slapped him.

"Don't come near me or my place again," he said. "I don't like Peeping Toms."

As he untied the reins on his saddle horse, he realized he still had his hat on his head. Quist hadn't touched him. Moving all those rocks had done some good.

Chapter Fifteen

Snow was falling on the street outside. Passing horses left their imprints, and carriage wheels left pairs of dark traces against the hard surface below. Lane sat at the window of the café, waiting, as had become a habit he knew he should break.

All the way on the train, he knew he was headed for something important. Not having heard from Cora, he thought he might be having his last rendezvous with her. He also had to consider the possibility that he had already had the last meeting. Without putting too high a premium on it, he thought also that he might have had his final session of intimacy with her. As with last frost, a fellow did not know, until later, if the true last time had put in an appearance.

Whatever the case, he had done his part. He had come to Laramie prepared to take action, and part of his preparation entailed thinking about action itself. On one hand, a fellow needed to do something decisive so as not to feel powerless like before. He had to do what he could. On the other hand, he needed to recognize that some courses of action just pulled him in and got him caught up in the tangle so that he couldn't let go. He needed to keep himself from getting hooked too deep, from expecting results proportionate to his measures. After all, he reminded himself, he was dealing with two people, one by proxy, who got through life by not resolving things.

He waited an hour, then two. The daylight broadened without the sun coming out. People appeared on the street, went into buildings, stepped in and out of carriages.

Then he saw her. She was wrapped in a dark blue wool overcoat and hat, but he knew her form and movement. Cora.

She came into the café with very much the same air as he remembered from their last meeting at Emma's—resigned, somber, defeated. He did not touch her but pulled out a chair and helped her get seated.

"I don't know where we want to start," he said.

"Well, things haven't changed here."

"You mean, you haven't done anything more."

"No."

"We probably don't have a great deal to talk about, then. But I think it's good to have an opportunity to say things."

"Go ahead. I imagine you have something prepared."

"Not really. Just some general ideas. If you'd like to say something, I'd be happy to let you go first."

Her eyes, dark blue today, had a lost look to them as she spoke. "I know you find it hard to believe me, but I have loved you. And I have wanted to be with you."

He waited for her to go on, and when she didn't, he spoke. "But not enough to do what you would have to do to follow through. You said you weren't going to lose me this time, but by not doing anything, in a way you've chosen otherwise. Inaction has become a choice, by default."

"I suppose you're right."

"I know you don't want to lose me, but however hideous I see your life to be with this other fellow, it's apparent that you don't want to give that up. As we said before, you can't be two people at once, not indefinitely."

"I know. And I've ruined your life, not once but twice, trying to do that."

"No, you haven't. I brought it on. But I'm not going to let things linger at this point."

She brought her eyes to meet his. "You have a right to do something about it."

"I should think so. What it looks like is this. For all the time we've known each other, you've referred to this fellow, your husband, as Someone. Meanwhile, I've always been Mr. Nobody, a secret, something stuffed in the closet, something to lie about even when everyone knows better. I have tried to escape that definition. I have tried to believe that what we had between us was real."

"It was."

"But I never had the status of being out in the open, something to be taken seriously in the debate."

"That's my fault."

"Let's not worry about casting blame. I played along with all of it because I didn't want to lose you. But I can see that things are on the way out, and not just because the third party is forcing it."

She nodded.

"And my feeling is that however this thing ends will define what it has been. Right now the prospect does not look very flattering, but rather it has a low, sneaky character to it."

Her eyes met his again. "It has been more than that."

"I like to think so, but it's hard to change when the definition settles in. I can accept it." He looked out the window at the bleak day, then returned his gaze to her. "A man can put everything on the line and get shortchanged, and he can believe that at least he did his part. Then he can do the same thing a second time, with similar results, and he can believe again that at least he gave it his all. Whether it is really honor or not, or whether all honor has left, he has that to take refuge in. What I can say for myself is, I tried."

Her eyes were moist with tears on the brink. "I know you did. And I will always love you for it. I'm sorry for what I did to your life."

"You didn't do it by yourself, and to the extent that you did anything to me, I forgive you for it."

She wiped her eyes. "Thank you. That helps. But I still worry about what you're going to do with yourself after this."

"Don't worry. I'm older, and a bit worse for the wear perhaps, but I've got plenty of life left in me."

She took a deep breath. "I don't suppose there's much more to say, then. I should be going anyway."

She pushed away from the table and stood up. He rose from his chair and took her by both hands. "Good-bye, Cora."

"Good-bye, Lane. I've loved you more than you can know."

He found it hard to speak. "I've loved you, too. And I tried."

"I know."

Then she was gone, her form disappearing in the light falling snow.

He went up to his room and packed his things. It was well before noon, and he was done here. He was not going to go back to see her house, or her window, nor was he going to wait to see her shadow on the shade. In the words of a book that had moved him more than once, he saw no shadow of another parting with her.

Walking down the street with a bag in each hand, he passed the shop where on more than one occasion he had seen an empty apothecary bottle on display. For no reason he could assign, he wanted to buy the bottle. He went inside, paid fifty cents, and walked out with it in his pocket.

Closer to the station, he paused at the sight of two young women inside a shop. It looked like a dress shop, and he thought they might work there, as they were not wearing coats or carrying handbags. He appreciated their shapes at the same time he realized they were beyond his reach. He was too old now to interest young women like them anymore. From that thought he moved on to imagine clumsy, oafish men who might never have had an attractive woman willing to share her intimacy, and he decided he had better be happy with what he had had and with what he had left.

On the train ride back, he had plenty of time to think things over. Outside the train window he saw the trees and rocks he had seen many times, and he realized he might not come this way again for quite some time. Everything he saw seemed detached; he had a numb feeling, as if he had gone through a bereavement. He did not yet feel free, but he knew he would find life out ahead of him.

For right now, any ending was a good ending. People like Cora and McGee could leave things hanging, but he couldn't. Cora must have learned it from her husband as a technique. Perhaps without knowing she did it, she practiced the method both ways to control men's lives, although, oddly, she could not control her own. Odd indeed. For as much as McGavin might think he was controlling everything, in the end he loomed as a pathetic figure, a cheap crook contriving to thwart his wife from doing things he hated but could not change.

As for himself, he had gotten something settled, something accounted for. As he had seen, people who were driven to have things acknowledged, satisfied, recorded, or ratified were not always that lucky. He didn't need the flamboyant ending of arsenic or the guillotine—just some kind of resolution.

It required letting go. He felt it in his organs, in his muscles, in his bones. He could not worry about the other spur or what became of the stone. Nor could he let himself care about sorting the truths from the half-truths from the lies. He had gone past the point of trying to get everything clarified; he saw no future to make the effort matter.

What did matter, what made it all worthwhile from beginning to end, was going to ask Emma where she lived. He could see it now. That was how in the second go-around he had gotten an answer to the question that got left hanging the first time. He could be satisfied with that.

The snow had cleared by the time he reached Willow Springs. A few inches of it lay on the ground, melting wherever a rock or a mound of dirt rose up. He rode through town, not caring who saw him, and tied up in front of the Last Chance Saloon. After a beer with Tom Sedley, he checked into a room in Rox Barlow's hotel. He took a hot bath, washing away the film and grime from his travel. Then he knocked on Madeline Edgeworth's door.

"She didn't leave him, did she?" Madeline stepped aside to let him in.

"No," he said as he took off his hat. "How did you know?"

"I saw you ride into town over an hour ago. And you wouldn't have knocked on my door otherwise."

"Balm for the soul. I'm glad you were here."

"So am I." She smiled as she took his hat. "It does me good to do you good."

"You're not as self-interested as you try to seem."

"My seeming so is for your benefit, too."

Lane decided not to spend the night. It would take more trouble to stable the horses and rig them out again in the morning than it would to ride to his place and be done with it now. As for his room rent for the night, it was like everything else. Already spent and didn't matter.

He carried his bag down to the hitching rail and tied it on the packhorse with the other bag. Late afternoon was shading into evening as he cinched his load and headed out of town for the breaks. He pulled on his wool gloves and settled his hat onto his head.

As he passed the last houses on the north edge of town, he saw a rider angle out across the plain toward the trail ahead of him. Lane recognized the posture and the compact form. Collier must have been looking out for him all afternoon from the blacksmith shop.

The man was riding a tall, dark horse, which he turned and brought to a standstill when he reached the trail. Lane felt his stomach tightening as he rode closer. It would not do to try to avoid a meeting; it would not resolve anything, and it would make him look like a coward.

"Back from your travels?" came the taunting voice.

"I don't see where it's any of your business."

"It's my business to teach you a lesson, and it seems you haven't learned it yet."

In that moment, Lane realized Cora would not have told her husband that anything had ended, especially since they had not recognized its existence. Thus it would be quite a while until Collier found out anything. Just as well that way.

"I don't think it's any of your business what I've learned or haven't learned," Lane said.

"Maybe it is."

"Then maybe I should tell you one thing I've learned. It's too bad people are willing to carry water for someone else. Kind of a dirty job. Filth by proxy. But maybe you like it."

"You've always been a smart one. Get off your horse, or I'll slap you in the face with this." Collier held up a coiled rope and nudged his horse forward a step.

Lane felt unsteady as he swung down from the saddle, put his gloves in his pocket, and set his hat on the pommel. Collier had ground-hitched his horse and left his hat and coat on the snow nearby.

"Come on," he snarled.

"You're the water carrier."

Collier came at him, swinging, and glanced a blow off his cheekbone. Lane punched back and felt the bristly skin of Collier's cheek. Collier backed up half a step, then came in with a left and a right. Lane took both punches to the head but managed to connect once before Collier got out. Then with a burst forward he took the fight to his opponent, hitting him not very hard but enough to make him stand back and take measure. Collier came forward in short steps, throwing punches that Lane blocked with his forearms. Then Lane shot a left jab and felt the nose and mustache and lip give way to his knuckles. He swung twice more, connecting, while Collier's punches fell short. It occurred to him that he had the reach on his opponent. He assumed Collier figured it out as well, for the shorter and more powerful man came at him in a rush, swinging punches like a brawler. Lane stiff-armed him with a punch and tried to step aside, and then they both went down in a tumble. Lane scrambled up and Collier came at him, grabbing his legs. Lane punched downward, twice, at the bulletlike head and then broke free.

Collier came to his feet but not very fast. Lane's left knuckles hurt, and he thought he might have landed a pretty good blow on the last punch. Collier put up his fists but did not move forward.

"Come on," he said, "you backdoor sissy."

They went at it again, trading a half dozen blows each, until Lane felt himself land a good one on the side of Collier's neck below his ear. Collier stood back and wavered, keeping his fists at chest height.

Lane spoke first. "I've had enough if you have. I don't think we're going to change anything."

"We'll see about that."

"Like I told your pal Quist, don't come around me or my place. From now on I'm fighting, and it's not going to take much."

"You still need to learn your lesson."

"I told you, it's none of your business what I've learned. As for the woman, whatever she might have done, she did it of her own free will, and no amount of bullying from a thief and forger is going to change that."

"What do you mean by that?"

"Go ask him. Tell him I told you to ask about the baby, and what he did to his wife in the house you built for him. Then see how proud you are to do his dirty work. But leave me alone. I'm done with you and your errands."

When he awoke to the gray walls inside his tent, he felt once again as if someone had died. Events of the previous two days came back to him, and he knew life was going to be different from now on.

As he rolled out of bed, he felt stiff and sore all over. Probably not a bad price for a standoff.

He got a fire going in the circle of rocks outside. As he waited for it to burn down to coals, he went into the tent and loaded the .38 he had gotten from Elbert. Then he took it and the blue bottle out into the morning.

Finding a dirt bank where he could stand back level at thirty yards, he set the bottle on a blanket of snow. Then he got into position and took his shots. He missed the first two, and on the third he shattered the bottle.

He put the pistol away and brought out the letters she had written this time around. After tossing them onto the coals, he crouched and poked at them with a stick as he watched them burn. Then he took from his pocket the one thing he had left—the locket that held her hair. He didn't begrudge her anything; he could keep this.

Sitting by the fire and looking out over the vast country, he had no misgivings. Poetic wisdom had it that a person could hope for one great love in this life. There didn't seem to be anything wrong with believing that, especially if personal experience seemed to bear it out.

But that didn't mean he couldn't love again. This feeling of bereavement would pass, and the great thing he believed in might come his way again. He, for one, was not dead yet.

He opened the locket and then closed it. He wouldn't need to look at it very often. After his long lone winter of wondering whether their love was something to lie about or something real, he felt he had his answer. It was both.